Out of Sorts

Out of
Sorts

Out of Sorts

Aurélie Valognes

Translated by
WENDELINE A. HARDENBERG

amazon crossing

Text copyright © 2014 Aurélie Valognes
Translation copyright © 2015 Wendeline A. Hardenberg

Previously published as *Mémé dans les orties* by the author via the Kindle Direct Publishing Platform in France in 2014. Translated from French by Wendeline A. Hardenberg. First published in English by AmazonCrossing in 2016.

Published by AmazonCrossing, Seattle

www.apub.com

Amazon, the Amazon logo, and AmazonCrossing are trademarks of Amazon.com, Inc., or its affiliates.

ISBN-13: 9781503950375
ISBN-10: 1503950379

Cover design by Kimberly Glyder

Printed in the United States of America

For Laetitia

Prologue

Skipping Town

December 2012

Slumped on his suitcase, Ferdinand Brun, age eighty-three, help-lessly surveys his apartment, which he is leaving forever. He who hates moving. Who hates communal living. Who hates people. How did it come to this?

His heart aches.

He takes a deep breath: the scent of mothballs fills his nostrils. The familiar fragrance soothes him. He's going to miss that smell, and the brown wallpaper with huge flowers, too, even though he never liked it.

He's grown accustomed to all these things—his furniture covered with sheets, his books stowed in plastic bags, sheltered from the dust. From time. From life.

Ferdinand has lived as a recluse for years—no friends, no family nearby. This is his fault, in a way. Throughout his life, though, he's made his choices, alone. Rarely the right ones. Always dictated by grudges or impulses. He's never changed course, nor admitted when he's wrong. His weaknesses, his mistakes, or just his feelings—he's always kept them to himself. "A real Aries!" as his grandmother would say.

So how could he have allowed a stranger to ensnare him and influence his fate? He hates to be told what to do—at his age, no less. And what's more, he'll never be able to stand living so far from his home.

Where he's going, he knows they'll try to infantilize him, to change him into Old Pappy Marshmallow. They can't fool him! And then there will be all those old harpies . . . No. He's had it with women!

Dressed warmly, Ferdinand has been waiting for his taxi for more than twenty minutes.

He searches his memory for the exact moment his fate started to get away from him. It all began right here, three years earlier. Right from the get-go, he and the neighbor ladies didn't gel. And exactly one year ago, the situation deteriorated, though he doesn't know why. Ferdinand is in the midst of remembering, when the telephone rings in the apartment. It takes him a moment to realize the ringing is for him. He stands abruptly, staggering, then picks up and hangs up in one sharp movement.

"It boggles the mind. Heaven forbid you be left in peace in your own home. Always somebody volunteering to be a pain in the ass, and today, no less." Ferdinand tears the telephone cord out of the wall and returns to his post in the entryway.

At no point does he think this call could be important. At no point does he consider it could be the taxi driver. At no point is Ferdinand aware that this phone call could have changed his life if he'd only listened to what the person at the other end of the line had to tell him, that it could have kept him from leaving.

No. Lost in his thoughts, Ferdinand muses that perhaps it isn't too late to stop everything. Doesn't one always have a choice? He could escape, lie low: his specialty. And if he doesn't go, what would happen? He will just be his usual self, predictable in his unpredictability. After all, isn't he the cantankerous old man who, as recently as last New Year's, terrorized his neighbors and laid down the law in his apartment complex? Isn't he still the man with the troubled past? The one everybody runs away from. The one they've dubbed the *serial killer*. There's bound to be a way out. He just has to find it. And not look back.

Chapter One

Turning Ugly

Eleven Months Earlier: January 2012

Things started to go wrong for Ferdinand when he moved into the apartment complex, two years earlier. After a divorce that had left him bitter, he'd moved into the left-hand side of the second floor of Building A in the apartment complex situated at Eight Rue Bonaparte. Built in the fifties, the well-maintained complex stood at the end of a street lined with hundred-year-old plane trees, in a tranquil little town. The walls of cut stone, the elegant black iron gate, and the lovely courtyard full of flowers between Buildings A and B always left the old man indifferent. As did the path lined with hollyhocks that wound around the little patio to the vegetable patch and the trash area.

At Eight Rue Bonaparte, all was quiet. Everyone enjoyed a peaceful existence. The residents were comfortable. It was an apartment complex without drama. The buildings had always housed around ten families; over time, the parents had watched their children leave the nest. Since then, single older ladies remained, in apartments grown too large for them. In the small courtyard, the only sound was the purring of Mrs. Berger's cat; or the singing of the canaries belonging to the concierge, Mrs. Suarez; or else the noises of her Chihuahua's greedy chewing as he gulped down his mistress's biscuits.

Every day after lunch you could also hear the cackling from a throng of old ladies who sat at tables on the patio, gossiping in the sun, hot beverages cradled in their hands. They spent hours gabbing, swapping the latest stories, solving all the world's problems—a tradition established decades ago.

All these people seemed made to live together. Never a voice raised, never a sound louder than the television. It was their heaven on earth.

But that was before.

Before the arrival of the disrupter. The antagonizer. A man. Alone. An octogenarian whose mysterious past and bizarre behavior immediately alarmed the residents of Eight Rue Bonaparte.

In the two years he'd lived on the second floor of Building A, across from Mrs. Claudel, Mr. Brun had imposed a reign of terror. The grandmothers tolerated the fellow's aggression as best they could—his inability to make an effort at community life. Not to mention his dog. A monster—a Great Dane. Together, this man and his dog had disturbed the tranquility of the premises. *Their* tranquility.

Everything escalated several months ago, after word spread of the death of Louise, the apartment's original owner and Ferdinand Brun's ex-wife. War was declared against the old man. From then on, behind those seemingly peaceful walls, the united residents plotted to rid themselves of their unmanageable neighbor. The cold war was over. The direct confrontation would begin—crueler, but more effective. All orchestrated by Mrs. Suarez, an iron-fisted woman who had been the apartment complex's concierge for more than thirty years.

Chapter Two

Holding a Grudge

Mrs. Suarez, age fifty-seven, is always elegant. In order to perfect the forced smile she aims at the little people (the mailman, the garbage men, the gardener), Mrs. Suarez maintains impeccable oral hygiene. Three daily cleanings of three minutes each, with an electric toothbrush, harsh mouthwash, resonant gargling, and then finishing off with dental floss. With all that hard work, it's a shame Mrs. Suarez constantly purses her lips and frowns, as busy as she is keeping an eye out for the smallest misstep by her fellow human beings.

Some residents have gotten used to her supervision and obey the rules. That's the case with Mrs. Joly, Mrs. Berger, and Mrs. Jean-Jean, subservient residents faithful to Mrs. Suarez. Mrs. Claudel, a superactive nonagenarian whose good breeding no longer needs to be proved, poses no problem, either. The other residents, however, have been more difficult to train. As soon as someone passes by her special concierge *loge* holding a trash bag, for instance, Mrs. Suarez follows. At the slightest deviation in sorting—a banana skin in the mixed-waste bin rather than the compost, for example—she picks up the intercom straightaway and rings their bell, or sticks a Post-it note on their door.

Yes, Mrs. Suarez does a thankless job, with very little recognition, but oh, how useful she is to the community. Without her, the apartment complex would go to wrack and ruin. But do the residents of Eight Rue Bonaparte realize it? Are the neighbor ladies aware of their good fortune in having Mrs. Suarez for a friend? And her husband, that good-for-nothing—shouldn't he thank her for living in this lovely apartment complex and finally being someone because of her?

For at Eight Rue Bonaparte, Mrs. Suarez is the mistress of the house, having inherited her position in the loge from her mother. She struts around the courtyard, does inspections, and keeps the various deliverymen and gardeners moving. She loves that things go quickly, that the chores get crossed off her list, so she can return to her post.

From her loge, Mrs. Suarez monitors the life of every resident. Outings, visits—she knows everything, knows everyone's habits. It's even rumored she logs everyone's quirks in a black notebook. She almost never leaves her post, where, with her sewing machine, she fashions little coats for Rocco, her Chihuahua. It's with regret that she leaves her loge twice a day to take out the trash and distribute the mail. The longest absence is when she deposits letters on doormats, which takes her exactly fifteen minutes.

Mrs. Suarez loves punctuality. If the mailman is late, she lets him know it. Even if those fifteen minutes are during off-peak hours—that is, when activity is at its lowest—Mrs. Suarez might still miss an infraction or an interesting movement. And she can't count on her husband, who refuses to pick up the slack and log those precious minutes, hiding behind his weak excuse that he thought he wasn't allowed to set foot in *his lady's loge*.

When Mrs. Suarez drops the mail on a doormat, she does so as quickly as possible and rarely accompanies her rounds with a "Hello." Though she is a gossip, she can't allow herself to be so all the time, and especially not with everyone.

And then there's Mr. Brun.

Mrs. Suarez hates Mr. Brun. She's hated him since the minute he and his dog set foot in her apartment complex. What with his not saying "Hello," cigar smoking in the common areas, never-sorted trash, and vacuum cleaner running during her cigarette break in the courtyard. She's convinced he performs some sort of mischief during her daily fifteen-minute absence, just to needle her. She's never been able to catch him in the act, but she's working on it.

The hollyhocks are thriving all around the courtyard, except under Mr. Brun's balcony. She'd bet her fur coat he waters them with weed killer. The lightbulbs in the common areas on the old man's floor blow out every month. And every time she does her mail rounds, the stairs are wet and slippery. Not to mention the enormous piles of dog waste across from the apartment complex, near the school. She'd bet they're from his filthy mutt. Though she can't stand Mr. Brun, she hates his dog even more—a colossus that frightens Mrs. Berger's cat, her own beloved Chihuahua, and above all, her poor canaries. Last year, six of them died of fear, because of the *beast*. The veterinarian couldn't confirm it, but she's certain of it.

To avoid being seen as vulgar, Mrs. Suarez accompanies the mail she deposits on the octogenarian's doormat every day with a "Hello, Mr. Brun." The barbarian has never answered her! Never, even though he's on the other side of the door, staring at her through the peephole. But she persists because she's sure her "Hello" antagonizes him.

It won't continue like this, though. Mrs. Suarez vowed as much after the death of her favorite bird. As the head of the apartment complex, she will take appropriate action. So with the help of her acolytes, she has hatched a plan to make Mr. Brun leave. It's what the ladies discuss every day in the courtyard during their vitamin D and nicotine break, after Mrs. Suarez's private lunch with the one o'clock news' handsome anchorman, while the noise of the vacuum cleaner prevents the old man from catching a single word.

Chapter Three

Jinxed

Ferdinand Brun is going deaf. It doesn't bother him much—he has no one to make conversation with anyway. But since he's a hypochondriac, he's already imagining the worst—complete hearing loss, like Mozart. Or was it Beethoven? He can't quite remember anymore.

Mr. Brun hasn't had much luck in life. It started out badly, and it wasn't really his fault. He was born on Friday the thirteenth. His mother did all she could to keep him in a few more hours, but she was able to ascertain the disappointing masculinity of her unwanted offspring twenty minutes early. The new mother then decided to say the birth had taken place on the fourteenth, as was the custom back then to ward off the evil eye, though Ferdinand eventually learned the truth.

But the bad luck continued to pursue Ferdinand Brun. His mother died two years later, following the birth of his little sister— herself born dead. Next, his grandmother, who raised him after his mother's death (he never knew his father), died at the hospital from the flu, though she had come for a broken leg. Finally, his wife, who took advantage of him and his salary for forty years, ran off with the first comer as soon as he retired from the factory.

Bad luck may not have had everything to do with it, though, as Ferdinand isn't the easygoing type. He runs on a different voltage, with a logic all his own, leaving him nearly incomprehensible to ordinary people.

For example, he's not about to risk losing his parking spot just to go refuel—he'll carry the empty jerry cans to the pump at the other end of the street and bring them back to his car instead. His furniture is still in its protective covers. And though he has new things neatly arranged in his wardrobe, he continues to wear his too-big trousers with the worn-out seams, his holey underpants, and the perforated wallet that could cause him to lose his credit card, if he'd resign himself to adopting that method of payment. In short, Ferdinand is thrifty—certainly with regard to property, but particularly to feelings. The only one who has ever mattered to him, the only one he loves, the only one who has never abandoned him, is Daisy. His dog. The most loyal. With her, everything is simple. No tricks. No coercion. No emotional blackmail. No need to furnish kind gestures or sweet nothings. That right there is the problem with everybody, but especially with women.

What's worrisome is that Daisy didn't come home last night. She wasn't tied to her usual post when he left the bakery, and she didn't join him for lunch, or for dinner, or to spend the night at his side. It's the first time this has happened. To disappear like that . . .

Ferdinand hovers around the telephone. He's not going to call the police, though. He hates cops. And it's too soon to be plastering her photo along the street. Ferdinand is worrying himself sick. Daisy is his last reason to live. In any case, at eighty-two years old, he has nothing else to do.

Chapter Four

Treated Like a King

Daisy has not returned. Ferdinand roamed the streets all day and into the night, called her name until his voice grew hoarse, wore his eyes out staring out the window, and couldn't sleep a wink. With a stool tucked under his rear, he is now riveted to the peephole, witness to the comings and goings of his neighbor across the way—a rickety old bat who puts on bourgeois airs with her Mary Poppins hairdo and whose wooden cane could hide a bit of alcohol, maybe to sip while waiting at the bus stop.

***

Like all Saturday mornings, it's a flurry of activity around Beatrice Claudel's apartment. She goes in, she goes out, ever more laden with packages, bags, boxes. Like every Saturday, she has one, some, or all of her grandchildren over for lunch. And she insists every-thing be spic-and-span. The house, the meal, the conversation. At ninety-two years of age, she wants to prove she's a granny who keeps up with the times—energetic and, above all, in great shape. Which isn't far from the truth, a few little health glitches aside. Of course, the old lady has a bit of difficulty understanding when everybody talks at once, but she isn't about to pop off tomorrow. She gladly trades her cane for a motorized cart when she does her shopping, since it happens to be "extremely convenient," as she says. Her eyes work much better since her cataract operation—the *Figaro*'s newsprint even changed from yellow to white like magic! In order to read, she still puts on her big round glasses, which she doesn't lose anymore since her grandkids gave her a very chic lanyard.

Beatrice Claudel is doing well—very well, even.

Today she's invited one of her grandsons, his wife, and their ten-month-old son. She's planned to cook braised chicken with mustard, her grandson's favorite, complemented by a good Côtes-du-Rhône she bought in a case of six at the last wine expo.

Everything is prepared. The Le Creuset casserole has been simmering for nearly two hours, the carrots and onions are cara-melizing, the table is set. This time, Beatrice has placed her pillbox next to her wineglass. She no longer leaves her medications on the table, after her bridge friend's grandson came to lunch and thought he'd add an olive to his plate . . . Thankfully, it was just a vision supplement.

Beatrice sits down in her armchair by the window, takes out her iPad, and opens Facebook. She wants to learn about her grandson's latest activities. This week, he made a business trip to Italy, ate at a fancy restaurant, and watched a reality TV show she hasn't heard of yet. As for her granddaughter-in-law, she's raving about their little one's new teeth and just finished reading this year's Goncourt Prize–winning novel. Beatrice checks her library for the last book they read in her book club, the one that lost the Renaudot Prize for whatever. She puts it on the table in the entryway, so she doesn't forget to offer it to her granddaughter-in-law. They have the same taste in literature, so she should like this one.

She goes to sit back down but gets right back up to put the appetizers on an earthenware platter. She picks the blue-green one her grandchildren gave her last Christmas. She also puts on the necklace she got for her birthday. 11:43 a.m. Beatrice even has time to take out the trash. The bag is full, mainly with stale bread.

"Oh, my God! The bread . . . I completely forgot to buy some. Do I have time to get more? Yes, plenty. But what if they get here early?"

***

Ferdinand watches his neighbor from across the way come back into the hall in a panic and rush back into her apartment. He doesn't know what could have frightened her that much in the trash area. Perhaps she, too, heard of that horrific true story about a murdered man cut up and disposed of, day after day, piece by piece, via a garbage chute? He'd read all about it in a Pierre Bellemare book. *Grim story*, thinks Ferdinand. He'll have to tell it to that silly old goose Mrs. Suarez, who loves snooping around the trash area so much.

Ferdinand's hindquarters are starting to hurt. *Look, there's the old hag coming out of her apartment, wearing an overcoat. That's unusual: she's going to be late.* Ferdinand twists to see her go down the stairs. The old man takes the opportunity to stretch his legs in the kitchen. He fills a saucepan with cold water. Ferdinand has never used the hot water faucet—not for cooking, not for washing himself. He boils the water. It's out of the question to pay for hot water from the building! Ferdinand is looking for the saucepan lid when he hears the sound of the cane on the stairs. In his slippers, he shuffles over to his stool and sits back down. The little lady is laboriously climbing the stairs. She's certainly not young anymore. *Much older than me*, thinks Ferdinand. All of a sudden, she turns and heads in his direction. Ferdinand stiffens. She takes a deep breath and knocks on his door. *What nerve!*

A husky voice says, "Mr. Brun, open up. It's Mrs. Claudel."

Mrs. Claudel. He's never bothered to learn her name.

"Mr. Brun, I'm sorry to insist, but I have news about your dog. Open up, please."

"*Daisy!* They've found Daisy!" Ferdinand exclaims, opening the door wide.

"I'm so very sorry, but I'm afraid the news isn't good."

"You found her? Yes or no?" says Ferdinand.

"Mrs. Suarez, our concierge, will be able to tell you more. She's downstairs with your dog's body. I'm really sorry, Mr. Brun."

Beatrice takes the old man by the arm and leads him down the thirteen steps separating him from his darling.

Chapter Five

Miserable as Sin

For two days Ferdinand has been shut away in his home, huddled in his bed in the fetal position, surrounded by crumpled tissues. He doesn't want to get up or go out. To go where, anyway? Everything would remind him of Daisy. He'd end up by the vegetable garden where Daisy used to relieve herself on the neighbor ladies' tomatoes, or by the house where a pug would sit up and safely bark at her from behind his gate.

The silence in the apartment is oppressive. His old habits now seem senseless. He no longer feels like doing anything, not even eating, just like when he got divorced. He still forces himself to swallow some expired preserves. He throws up a little, but he doesn't feel well anyway. Death by food poisoning or something else—what does he care? Besides, he's feeling pressure in his chest, a weight that hinders his breathing. That sense of suffocation doesn't leave him, as if to fill the void left by Daisy.

Though sadness and solitude are his new companions, there is still room for an even more invasive feeling: anger. Ferdinand cannot resign himself to accept the theory of an accident. There must be someone to blame, someone on whom to focus his hatred. Daisy was so young, barely four years old. And she was the sweetest creature there was—she wouldn't have hurt a fly. She'd never even gone near the concierge's canaries. Even the attacks by the neighbor's cat, the one in 2B, didn't affect her. She'd just side-eyed it with panache.

It's incomprehensible. Daisy had never tried to escape when he tied her up to the post outside the market. She'd had exemplary patience. And if the knot in her leash had come undone, she wouldn't have run away. At worst she would have gone home, and for that she had no need to cross the street. She knew the route by heart. They walked it every day. So why? Why had she disappeared? Why had she crossed the road all alone?

What if this is a case of mistaken identity? What if *he* is the target? Once again that damned bad luck that takes away his women, one after the other, has struck.

Ferdinand bellows, not realizing he's talking out loud, "If you had to take somebody, it should've been me, not her! What am I supposed to do now? And what am I going to do with my darling? Cremation or burial?

"And what about your things, Daisy? I can't throw them out, not your chew bone, or your threadbare old pillow. I'll never be able to replace you. I miss you so much, my darling. I think this is the end—my end. There's nobody left to say hello to me at the door in the morning, to make me take a walk and go buy lunch. Nobody left to look at me with those sweet eyes, or disapproving ones when I rake a TV host over the coals.

"I'm not anything anymore. Just a grub. I don't even have a picture of you. Just memories, and mirages, too, when I think I see you in the distance. Sometimes I tell myself that all this is just a terrible nightmare, that the telephone will ring and they'll tell me about a regrettable mistake. And you'll be there, alive, tail wagging, happy to see me again. Other times, I dream I wake up and you're there, we go out for a walk by the lake where you loved watching the mallards so much. I've thought a lot about it. I don't want this life without you. I don't want to see anybody anymore. I don't want fake sympathetic looks from my damned neighbors. I know what they're thinking deep down: 'Serves him right! He had it coming. He should've been nicer. You only get what you deserve!' But you didn't deserve that.

"I don't understand: if there's a God, how could he let this happen? Yes, I know I don't believe in God, but I don't know how to imagine what comes next. I guess we both knew what was coming. The calendar's just sped up, that's all. See you in a few days. I just need to square away the last details, my Daisy."

Chapter Six

Pushing Up Daisies

On a lovely winter's day, after a week of talking to himself and rejecting reality, Ferdinand rouses from his stupor. It's a lovely day to go for a walk. A lovely day to make a fresh start.

Ferdinand finishes cleaning his nails. Dark green corduroys have taken the place of his old worn-out pants. The creases are sharp. He puts on clean underwear and socks without holes. The old man is dressed to the nines: hair combed, face freshly scrubbed, shoes shined. He's ready. And precisely on time. He writes a few words in his notebook and puts on his overcoat. *The walk will be pleasant*, he tells himself. In the courtyard, the birds chirp at him in greeting. Blackbirds, most likely.

Outside, he looks at the world around him. The Earth didn't stop turning in Daisy's absence. Everyone goes about his or her business: the baker makes change, the florist prepares a bouquet, the bus driver waves to his colleague. Everything seems lighthearted.

The clock strikes ten, and Ferdinand looks at his watch: right on time.

***

On Rue Garibaldi, a woman sits at the bus stop with a newborn nestled in her arms. An old lady begins to offer advice: "If I may, since, you know, I'm a grandmother . . ." The young mother simply nods, smiling. All of a sudden, she stands up and screams. The old lady also stands up suddenly. The bus . . . it was pulling up when . . . a man, an older gentleman . . .

The baby cries. A crowd gathers. The bus has stopped. The bystanders, like bamboo shoots, lean this way and that for a better view. The young mother is on the phone: help is on the way. She bounces her baby to calm him. Crows settle in the trees along the street. People whisper and speculate.

EMTs arrive at the scene. They move the passersby aside and bring in the stretcher. Everything goes very quickly. A body is lifted from the ground and taken away. There's blood—on the victim's overcoat, on the pavement—in front of the bus—and a little farther up on the sidewalk. The ambulance leaves the scene. The passengers from the bus are asked to exit the vehicle, and the bystanders are asked to be on their way.

At the corner of Rue Bonaparte and Rue Garibaldi, there's nothing left to see. Just a police officer who has taken up position near the large dark spot, keeping away the crows that are waiting for the lane to be free. Next to the brown stain are minute shards of glass from a watch. Mr. Brun's watch.

Chapter Seven

A Bitter Pill to Swallow

There's a very thick white fog. Noises, too, in the distance. Noises that repeat, endlessly.

Where am I? Am I already there? I can't see anything. I feel like I'm rolled in cotton. Like the inside of a cloud. I hear voices, like a choir, and those pings, those electronic sounds. Beeps. Beeps like the cash register at the mini-mart. But where am I?

Ferdinand's mouth feels full of paste, with an aftertaste of iron. His tongue passes over his teeth, one by one. A hole. The lower left canine has vanished. A bottom tooth is missing!

I've always had all my teeth! All except the wisdom teeth. Could this be a toll of some kind? I don't understand. I can't see anything. I don't recognize my mouth, or my body. I want to holler but no sound comes out. Yoo-hoo! Is anybody there? Help me!

As if out of nowhere, a blurry white shape appears, without distinct features. The long immaculate dress comes near and leans over. Then he hears a kind voice. "Mr. Brun. Everything's OK. You're with us now. You've certainly taken your time. You gave us quite the fright."

Ferdinand would like to nod, but a sharp pain shoots through his jaw.

"I forgot to introduce myself. I'm Dr. Labrousse. You have a guardian angel, Mr. Brun. If you weren't so tall and the bus's rearview mirror so low, that would have been the end of you. The bus would have hit you head on and crushed you. We get people less fortunate than you in here every day."

Rearview mirror. Bus. Fortunate?!

"Apart from the dislocated jaw, which we've put back in place, you're fine. Not the slightest fracture. Just a few scrapes and a missing tooth. A real miracle!" Ferdinand touches the lower half of his face. Dr. Labrousse continues, "Yes, we've put a bandage on to keep your jaw in place. You'll have to leave it there for another week."

Ferdinand begins to understand. "But if I'm not up there, where am I?"

"At Saintes Grâces Hospital. Fifth floor."

"But if I'm fine, why can't I see anything?"

"Don't worry, we put compresses around your eyes to keep the swelling down. They're obstructing your vision for the moment, but have no fear, we're going to take them off. I requested further analysis and the results are rare: diabetes, cholesterol, liver, and heart workup—it's all perfect! You have an iron constitution, Mr. Brun, and your heart is good as new. It's like it's never been used. I hope for the same when I'm your age. Don't change anything and you'll see a few decades more."

Still alive? Still around for more than ten years? Despite the doctor's pronouncements, Ferdinand is determined to finish what he started, as soon as he gets out of the hospital.

Chapter Eight

Not Out of the Woods Yet

No weapons, no hatred, no violence.

"Not a bad epitaph," Ferdinand muses aloud. "The problem is it doesn't apply to me," he concludes, immersed in the biography of Albert Spaggiari, a nonviolent thief.

"I'd need something more like, *Alone at last! No regrets, no tears, no psychobitches.* I don't know if they'll let me put *psychobitches* . . . Then again, if it's in the dictionary, they'd have no reason not to." Ferdinand grabs his dictionary, which is covered in dust. "So, under *P* we find . . . *pooch.* Hmm, not really a good time to bring that up again. *Ptarmigan* . . . ah, too far." He flips back and skims.

"Bah, it's not there! *Psychobitch* isn't in the dictionary. And it's the best one! Somebody's gonna have to explain to me why they put words in there nobody ever uses, like *psycholinguistics* or *ptomaine*. Maybe it's because my dictionary is too old. 1993. Didn't psychobitches exist back then, too? Fine, what's your advice, Daisy? Because ultimately this concerns you, too!" He turns toward an urn set on his desk.

"Oh, yeah, did you think I could leave without you? I'm going to request they bury the urn with me. Marion will make a fuss. Then again, if I'm paying, I'll do what I want!

"Come on, let's make an appointment with the funeral parlor. We're doing this! It ought to be put to use in no time. We're done with failed experiments like the bus. I've found a better way to rejoin you, Daisy. So where are the yellow pages?"

The telephone rings.

"What is with this phone only ringing when I want to use it?" Ferdinand grumbles as he picks up the receiver. "Yes? Who is this? Oh, Marion, it's you. Bad timing, I'm busy. Call back later."

"No, Papa. It's urgent. You have to listen to me. I have important things to tell you."

"You're just going to talk to me about your damned cop ex-husband again. Thanks, but I've had my fair share of your tales of woe. I'm not your shrink! Anyway, you should think about seeing someone. Don't they have shrinks in Singapore?"

"No, Papa, it's not about that. This isn't easy for me, but you've left me no choice. I'm sorry . . . At least before, there was Daisy. Her presence reassured me. If something happened to you, she would have let somebody know, one way or another. Now you're all by yourself there, you don't go out anymore, you don't bathe, your place is a mess, you eat badly, you're hostile with everyone. And you jump in front of buses!"

"Are you finished?"

"No. What will it be the next time? You're scaring me, Papa! And I'm too far away to take care of you."

"I'm not asking you to."

"Papa, you don't understand. I called a retirement home and we're in luck—they can take you in as soon as next month. You'll start off with a small room where you can have some of your own furniture, and later, you can move to a bigger room when—"

"What's all this about? Why should I go to a retirement home? It's out of the question, Marion! You can't get rid of me like that. And nobody decides for me! Period."

"Papa, I'd prefer other options as well, but you're a danger to yourself and others. If you'd at least give me a good reason to trust you, if you'd prove to me you wanted to change . . ."

"You don't change anymore at my age. It's too late. I am who I am. Take me or leave me."

"OK. End of discussion. You're going to a retirement home. They'll come pick you up on the first Monday next month. With Eric's help, if necessary."

"You're getting the police involved with this? I'd rather die than go to a retirement home. You'll have my death on your conscience, Marion!"

"Papa, this is to protect you from yourself. I love you and I don't want you to hurt yourself."

"Don't you think you're exaggerating? *Hurt myself?* A bus knocked me over and *I'm* suicidal? That's a good one!"

"Papa, prove to me you're making an effort and I'll stop the whole thing."

"Fine, I'll try, if I really have to . . ."

"Great, then I'll have someone come inspect your apartment, your refrigerator, and your hygiene. This person will report to me every month and if you've been rude to your neighbors, or you're neglecting yourself, or you're showing signs of self-destruction, I'm calling Eric so he can take you to the retirement home. I'll hold the reservation on your room just in case. Understand? I'm counting on you."

"Do whatever you want, my girl. Send whoever you want. I don't care. I have nothing to hide. And I told you, I'm not looking to die."

"I'm going to ask Mrs. Suarez to look after you, too."

"That was the only thing missing! That silly old goose? You couldn't find worse? She'll be delighted to play gestapo with me."

"Papa, promise me you'll cooperate."

"Mrs. Suarez can come sniff my armpits if she feels like it. She's totally welcome!"

"OK, that's enough. I'll call you in five days. By then, I'll have received the first report from the concierge. Love you, Papa!" Marion said, hanging up.

"Pff, that silly old goose will be eating out of my hand. And in less than ten days, she won't know what hit her."

Chapter Nine

That Takes the Cake!

Mrs. Suarez knows why people take her so quickly into their confidence. She exudes honesty. She can't help it—it's innate. She's a woman of principles, of values, and she knows how to show she's listening. Or perhaps it's a result of her perfume. Opium by Yves Saint Laurent. But she can't do anything about it if people are drawn to her.

In any case, Mrs. Suarez leaves nothing to chance. Even her hair is under control. Every evening, a blue net holds her peroxided curls in place, which has the advantage of discouraging any reckless carnal desire in her husband as effectively as a chastity belt.

After a night of heavy, dreamless sleep, thanks to the sleeping pills she takes more out of habit than need (her husband hasn't snored since the apnea operation), she heads to the bathroom, where the fixtures from the eighties and the lighting leave much to be desired.

She overpowders her olive complexion with Terracotta, then her eyelids with colored shadows that match her outfit. She finishes her eye makeup, mouth open wide, by coating her lashes with black Rimmel mascara. It's important to create an open look in order to highlight brown eyes: her cousin the beautician taught her that. She outlines her lips with a thick beige pencil, which has the dual benefit of giving her plump Pamela Anderson lips and also keeping the lipstick—generally of a brighter pink color—from spilling over into the furrows caused by many years spent taking energetic drags on her menthol cigarettes.

She largely avoids eyeliner on her upper lids, preferring to save that for special occasions, even if those are rare, with a plumber for a husband. She can't help but think how different her life would have been if she'd agreed to marry Marcel Cochard, who today serves as an accounting assistant at city hall. He was too ugly forty years ago, but now it wouldn't bother her so much.

Now what bothers her the most is that everyone believes she's Portuguese, given her last name. So she tries to clarify the situation with each newcomer before they reach their own conclusions—she is French, like her mother, Marianne. The only Portuguese in this scenario is her husband the plumber.

She never misses an opportunity to get decked out in all her finery: a fox fur coat inherited from her grandmother, who received it from her own grandmother; black leatherette boots; flashy jewelry at all her extremities—ears, wrists, and fingers—with the whole ensemble enhanced by oversized sunglasses to keep her curly hair back.

To perfect her nouveau riche style, she tucks her Chihuahua, Rocco, under her arm to prevent any tachycardia that might occur if he were to exert himself or encounter some cannibalistic animal. Voilà, Mrs. Suarez is ready. Ready to scrutinize the complex's trash and greet the mailman, among other things! Everyone would give first prize for beauty to the Little Miss Sunshine of Rue Bonaparte, more out of fear than for her resemblance to Paris Hilton—minus the hotel wealth, and including menopause and forty-five pounds in the rear.

In her work, she applies the same rigor as she does to her appearance, strictly following the techniques her mother taught her. And the student has surpassed the master, since adding her own rules.

Rule Number One: Everyone is prohibited from entering her loge, including her husband. He has the gift of making a mess wherever he goes, as evidenced by his workshop at the back of the apartment. In Mrs. Suarez's loge, as in her home, everything is square: not a speck of dust, nothing out of its place. A real model home, with a husband who just barely has the right to breathe, but who mostly slips away as soon as Mrs. Suarez has visitors.

The raspberry-colored sofa in the living room is her and Rocco's personal throne. Close to her couch is her thimble collection, religiously arranged in a locked glass cabinet. An air freshener, whose floral perfume irritates the throats of those unaccustomed to it, is plugged in to cover the *manly*—that is to say, *sweaty*—odor that emanates from the fabric on the sofa and even filters into her loge.

In the concierge's lair: sewing supplies, pictures of Rocco, *People* magazines. She loves to be on the cutting edge of fashion and caught up on the latest news. And on her little wooden desk, hidden from the view of passersby, is her famous black book. The tiniest details of everyone's life are recorded there, and, primarily, their lapses with regard to Rule Number Two.

Rule Number Two: Set the rules, make them known, and ensure they're respected by everyone. The notebook has a new section dedicated entirely to Mr. Brun. That troublemaker will pay for his misdeeds.

And now that she's been sent on a mission by Marion, Mr. Brun's life is in her hands. She feels as powerful as a child turning the garden hose on an anthill and watching the little creatures struggle to survive.

Rule Number Three: Impose the appropriate penalties when the rules are broken.

Chapter Ten

Going to Pot

It takes very little to disturb the peace at Eight Rue Bonaparte. When Ferdinand first moved into the apartment, he had yet to say anything, yet to do anything, and Mrs. Suarez already hated him. In elementary school, the concierge had been in the same class as Louise, Ferdinand's ex-wife. They had remained friends. And Ferdinand would be willing to bet it was Mrs. Suarez who pushed Louise to ask for a divorce. She'd never been shy about expressing her opinion of their twenty-five-year age difference. He wouldn't be surprised, either, if she'd visited Louise and her mailman on the Riviera. *That silly old goose is the type to roast topless all day at the beach.* In short, Mrs. Suarez must not have had a favorable view of the cuckolded husband's arrival at her apartment complex, and his moving into Louise's parents' apartment, no less—even if, technically, it now belongs to Marion.

In any case, after the icy stare Mrs. Suarez cast upon Mr. Brun the first time she encountered him with his dog, there was no way she could ever make up for her behavior—even if she'd wanted to. Ferdinand doesn't forget. He never forgets. He's quite vindictive. So being buddy-buddy with that silly old goose is out of the question! He knows all his misdeeds are veritable grenades. He takes perverse pleasure in tossing cobblestones into her pool of tranquility. Refusal to adorn his balcony with the "regulation" red geraniums; refusal to abandon the garbage chute in favor of five waste-sorting bins to be kept in his home; refusal to gossip with the neighbor ladies in the courtyard . . . His fate is in Mrs. Suarez's hands, and she will choose when to unleash everyone on the evil Mr. Brun.

Ferdinand is not easily impressed. Some bitter old woman with the IQ of a turkey isn't going to make him change his ways. In any case, it's the neighbor ladies who are afraid. One day, they found a book by Pierre Bellemare about the century's greatest serial killers—the pages full of annotations—in the trash. Ferdinand could see he'd struck a nerve! Their jitters lasted for weeks, during which the old man exulted every time they nervously said, "Hello, Mr. Brun," "Good day, Mr. Brun," "Everything all right, Mr. Brun?" "Can I do anything for you, Mr. Brun?"

So, if at first Ferdinand hadn't purposely antagonized his neighbors, he's since carefully plotted his next moves and taken perverse pleasure in making life unbearable for them. He does *everything* he can to make himself disagreeable. Ferdinand responds to their false friendliness with boorishness. He grunts or replies curtly with the most spiteful, impolite sentence he can think up. Or worse, he feigns deafness, ignoring the vile little things who dare to address him. And though he hates the smell of cigars and has never been a smoker, he lights up in secret every day so as to leave an odor of stale tobacco in the common areas, where smoking is *strictly* prohibited.

His hostility has become second nature, a way of life, of survival, even. Yes, survival, because Ferdinand resents growing old. Solitude, the decay of the body, all that is slowly killing him. The only activity Ferdinand has found to stave off boredom is being nasty so no one misses him when he goes.

This occupies his relentlessly similar days, but it entertains the neighbor ladies even more. They should thank him! Before, their conversations only revolved around the degenerate youth who no longer greet their elders and don't learn anything in school, or the yuppies who demand a bike park but drive around in 4x4s, who request a community garden but gorge themselves on out-of-season produce at restaurants, who call themselves "green" but can't manage to sort their waste correctly. *The yogurt cups don't go in the bin with the plastics, for crying out loud!*

With the coming inspections from Mrs. Suarez, Ferdinand has a vested interest in grinning and bearing it, but he's never been able to submit to decrees. When the old ladies of Eight Rue Bonaparte scrutinize Mr. Brun's smallest deeds and slightest gestures, Ferdinand can't help but make a comment or acerbic remark. It brightens his day. Like with Christine, his neighbor the hairdresser, for example.

Chapter Eleven

Splitting Hairs

The yellow plastic clock in the kitchen says 9:02.

"That foolish woman is late. As if I had nothing else to do today." The doorbell rings, accompanied by grumbling from Ferdinand as he opens the door.

"You're late! Did you get lost?"

Christine Jean-Jean, hairdresser and shampooer for the home hairstyling salon Hair Affair, lives in Apartment 2A, right above Ferdinand.

"Hello, Mr. Brun. No, I didn't get lost. I'm sorry, I thought I was on time."

The young woman barely has time to cross the threshold before Ferdinand turns and heads for the living room, where he sits down in a shapeless armchair, a copy of a satirical newspaper in his lap.

Ferdinand eyes her warily as she squints in the dim light of his apartment. Little does he know that Christine asked Mrs. Suarez to notify the police if she hasn't left his apartment by ten o'clock. Christine sits down next to Ferdinand and opens up her case, taking out shampoo, scissors, and a cape.

"By all means, take your time, we've got all day," Ferdinand says.

In order to serve the senior citizens at Eight Rue Bonaparte, Christine makes a few morning appointments before leaving for the salon. Her specialty is color. Ferdinand would say *all* the colors, including ones you won't find on the L'Oréal color chart. Her spectrum runs from royal blue to carrot orange, by way of eggplant purple and cotton candy pink. From his window, Ferdinand likes to admire the hairdresser's creations. Once the neighbor ladies have gathered in the little garden, you'd think you were at a gay pride parade!

But Ferdinand just needs a trim, so he gets a grip and, Christine's artistic talents aside, wills himself to ignore all her annoying little quirks. Like the way she talks constantly in that shrill voice, nattering on about anything and everything, never thinking about the meaning of the words coming out of her mouth. He also hates how she's "sorry" about every little thing, and how she darts fearful glances at him. Above all, Ferdinand can't stand how it's always *Mr. Brun* this, and *Mr. Brun* that. She can do all the bowing and scraping she wants—she's getting one hundred francs—that is, fifteen euros—and not a cent more. And that's only if she doesn't botch it.

"I'm ready to start, Mr. Brun. I set up as fast as I could, Mr. Brun. May I ask if today is a special day for you? Normally you don't call me in . . ."

Buried in his newspaper, Ferdinand pretends not to hear. Yes, this day is a big day for him, but like every year, no one will remember, let alone care. So this fool Christine can pack up her false sympathy, along with her scissors. It's April 13, Friday again! But Ferdinand is depressed. He doesn't have the heart to face another year. He doesn't even know why he wants to make himself presentable.

"How are you, Mr. Brun? I mean, since your accident . . . and especially your dog's death? I know that was hard for you. He was your only family, in a sense . . ."

With a seemingly clumsy but precise gesture, Ferdinand knocks over Christine's tools. He can't take it anymore, but she's barely started. And the way people keep saying "he" when talking about Daisy—it's unbearable!

Christine bends down to pick up the scissors while muttering, "Well, I doubt you ever shed a tear, let alone have a heart." Resuming her lighthearted tone, she says, "We can move to the sink, if you please, Mr. Brun."

"No need. I washed it last week."

"Are you sure, Mr. Brun? It would do you good."

"I said no. Would you prefer I say it in another language?"

"Very well, as you wish, Mr. Brun. So just a cut, then?"

"You're a bit slow on the uptake, Christine."

"Sorry, Mr. Brun. So how would you like it cut today?"

"Silently."

Chapter Twelve

Hard Knocks

After getting rid of Christine, Ferdinand looks at himself in the mirror. With his square jaw, steel-blue eyes, and this haircut that's too short on the sides, he looks like a soldier. And the neighbor ladies were already afraid of him. This is the last time he'll call on that amateur. One bright spot is that the bruises on his jaw have practically disappeared. He decides not to put on his bandage to go out. He's sick and tired of having an egghead, and besides, today is his birthday. Eighty-three years old. He decides to go for a walk, in spite of the menacing sky.

Lost in thought, Ferdinand doesn't realize he's been wandering for hours in the pouring rain. He's cold and no longer knows where he is. He was thinking about Daisy, about her cremation. He's tired. In his shopping bag is a small rectangular box containing the urn. He doesn't even know why he brought it with him; maybe to find a good place for her.

In a way, this was a good day to start over. The rain on his eyelashes is blurring his vision, and he's stomping along, when an enormous wave breaks over him and hits him like a cold slap. A car has just sped by through a muddy puddle. He turns to see if anyone observed the scene and is making fun of him. But no one seems to have witnessed it. Ferdinand looks down the road in search of the car. Maybe it was that little red one up ahead? He stares at the puddle as if he'll find a clue in it. The puddle is close to the sidewalk. Too close. The car shouldn't have gone through it—the lane is wide enough. The driver must have been in the middle of something else, sending a text or, if it was a woman, putting on makeup. Ferdinand isn't even annoyed—he's weary, resigned. It's one more sign he's been too long on this Earth, that his existence is nothing but a colossal joke.

The old man heads back up the street like a zombie, head tucked into his coat collar to keep the raindrops from beading on his neck. He's frightening to behold. Pitiful, too. His steps carry him back home. Ferdinand doesn't notice the little red car parked on the sidewalk across from his building. He also doesn't see the streaks of mud on the right fender. It never occurs to him that someone might have deliberately tried to humiliate him, or worse, kill him . . . before changing her mind.

Chapter Thirteen

Battle Stations

A couple of weeks later, Ferdinand wakes up groggy, having slept poorly. It's 8:20 in the morning, and he must have gotten at most an hour and a half of sleep. Exhausted, he abandoned his bed some time ago in favor of the living room couch, where he's rolled himself up in a thick, pilly blanket. As the sun comes up, he finally lets go and sinks into a heavy sleep, when a metallic noise rings out in the kitchen. "Daisy, get out of the kitchen right now! Daisy?"

Ferdinand concentrates. He hears the noise again. Then he realizes his eyes are shut, and he forces himself to open them. Again that sound. It's coming from the stairwell, not the kitchen. So it can't be Daisy . . . Then he remembers she's gone for good. This Daisy apparition was just a beautiful mirage. But the noise that pulled him from his dream is quite real. Ferdinand gets up, tottering to the entryway. Through the peephole, he discovers tons of boxes blocking his door. Several men are in the midst of carrying a sofa up the spiraling staircase, and at each landing the steel frame bangs against the walls. The racket is deafening.

"Be careful!" yells Ferdinand, more to himself than to be heard. "The paint will flake off again . . ." Bang! "Good God, be careful!" He knows the score: afterward—it'll be the owners who pay for these damned tenants who vandalize everything because they can't afford a moving company with a hydraulic lift. Ferdinand is beside himself. It's not even nine o'clock in the morning, he hasn't slept a wink, and this is the day these morons choose to make such a terrible racket?

"Can't they put a sock in it?" He lost Daisy just a few weeks ago. They could leave him in peace, for Pete's sake. He would have called the police to protest the disturbance, but after eight thirty in the morning, his request would lack legitimacy. People don't have respect for anything anymore. What if he needed to go out? Would he have to shove the boxes aside by himself? Climb over the furniture? At his age?

Ferdinand goes into the bathroom to put in earplugs (very useful on New Year's Eve and Independence Day) and settles in back on the couch. Suddenly, he remembers he got an ear infection the last time he used them. They weren't the cleanest things. Oh, well. He has to sleep. He wants to sleep.

But he can't manage it. The scraping right in front of his door, the movers' deep voices, their heavy steps, the moving of objects. It's impossible. He tosses and turns, gets annoyed, grumbles, gives up, and eventually gets up. Though all parking is prohibited in the courtyard, a moving truck is there. So somebody is moving into the building and nobody thought to warn the tenants of possible inconvenience? Who are these people?

Next to the truck, parked facing the other way, is a little red Ford, slightly dirty. Ferdinand knows this car. It's normally parked in front of the Hair Affair Salon, and the backseat is always full of flyers for styling products. It's Christine's car. Could she be leaving the building? To go where? Ferdinand would be willing to bet it's to follow a lover who will break her heart by never leaving his wife. Ah, these women who don't know how to make good decisions, and wait for men to do it for them!

"And to think I'm going to have to go outside to get any peace. Really, what kind of world are we living in?" Two options come to mind. The library or the church. At the library, the seats are more comfortable. But on a Saturday morning, they'll be taken over by little brats or, worse, their parents. Ferdinand doesn't like children, and he likes these new lax parents who refuse to give their kids the slightest spanking even less. The good-for-nothings are raising a generation of little emperors over whom—at barely three years old—they've lost all authority, and are therefore abandoning their snot-nosed brats' upbringing to others. In his day, that didn't fly. Not at school, not at home. And when the teacher reported his shenanigans to his grandmother, Ferdinand got a slap in front of his teacher (in addition to his usual smacks), and another thrashing at home, for the public shame. Ferdinand therefore behaved himself rather well. At least he was clever enough not to get caught too often.

If he weren't so deaf and so resistant to novelty, the old man could take refuge in a movie theater, but he hasn't seen anything on the big screen since *Don't Look Now . . . We're Being Shot At!* in 1966. A museum, a café, or a restaurant are pleasant hideaways, but they don't even occur to him as options. So he sets out for the church, a man who isn't the least bit God-fearing.

In order to leave, Ferdinand has to climb over the boxes on his doormat. As he lifts his leg, he tells himself that if he'd been an animal, he would have gladly relieved himself on one of these crates. On the ground floor, it's a jungle. The lobby is filled with pots overflowing with soil and jutting trees. If Ferdinand were better versed in horticulture, he would recognize a Japanese camellia, an oleander, an orange tree, a red maple, and several perennials. But what Ferdinand does know best, like a modern-day Attila the Hun, is weed killer, as his naked balcony and the poor hollyhocks underneath can attest.

"I hope they don't plan on putting all those trees above my place! All I need is for them to bring the balconies crashing down—onto my balcony!"

Upon arriving at the church, Ferdinand pushes open the heavy wooden door, enters without crossing himself, and sits down in a pew at the back of the nave. Nobody else is there. He enjoys his tranquility, even if the smell of incense bothers him—his ex-wife always lit a stick of incense after meals. After barely twenty minutes, Ferdinand shifts from one cheek to the other. It isn't very comfortable. He's cold, too, and hungry. It's 10:40, a bit early for a ham sandwich. He sighs. The day will be long. Very long.

All of a sudden, the wooden door opens and shuts heavily. Ferdinand glances up discreetly to see who's come to pray. But no one passes by. He senses a presence behind him. Ferdinand feels himself being watched, a very disagreeable sensation. He slowly turns around to find a stooped man wearing a raincoat standing to the left, near the entrance. He appears to be waiting for something or someone. Ferdinand hears the stranger's rhythmic wheezing. Each inhalation seems to scrape down the sides of his windpipe before working its way out through narrow, congested nostrils. Every breath is agony. On a normal day, Ferdinand would find it extremely annoying, but fatigue and solitude have gotten the better of him, and the hollow sound sends chills down his spine.

Ferdinand is on guard. He feels as if a crouching beast is preparing to pounce. He hopes someone comes in, even the priest, even if it means he has to go to confession. He could easily conjure up a few unorthodox tales to admit. His only objective is to not stay here alone with this psychopath. But no priest shows up, and no other charitable soul is on the horizon. Ferdinand summons the courage to stand up. Slowly, he heads for the door, as normally as possible, without glancing at the man.

Once he reaches the reassuring light of day, the evil demons are behind him.

***

At 2:30 p.m., having gulped down a sandwich made with stale bread, Ferdinand is shivering on a bench in the church square.

He hasn't dared return inside, dreading the presence of his chance companion. *I hate movers. I already hate these new neighbors who are forcing me to roam the streets like a bum.* Without even knowing his tormentors' identities, he almost misses the hairdresser. But a ray of hope makes him hold fast to the bench—Ferdinand knows how to welcome the new neighbors in turn, and thank them for this terrible day . . .

After more than five hours, completely exhausted, Ferdinand finally returns home. The moving truck has disappeared, but the green plants are still crowding the lobby, and the stairs are littered with scraps of cardboard. Still, someone did deign to clear the way to his door. Silence has returned. At last! Ferdinand collapses into his bed, determined to fall asleep as quickly as possible, when, all of a sudden, he hears a whimper. He forces himself to stay focused on his sleep and pulls the blanket up over his head.

"It's nothing," he says when, this time, a cry rings out from above his bed. *It can't be true . . . no, not that! I have to refocus. It'll stop. It has to stop.*

But it doesn't stop. Between 4:30 and 6:00 p.m., no relief. The cries of the new occupant of the bedroom upstairs have only ceased long enough for a bottle, too quickly drained. When Ferdinand gives up and leaves his bedroom to collapse into his armchair, he turns up the volume on the quiz show *Questions for a Champion* to cover up the incessant sniveling. The show, a favorite of everyone at Eight Rue Bonaparte, has already started. The "Four in a Row" round reveals a mystery category dear to Ferdinand: attack dogs.

"Ah, finally, something positive! I'm gonna get all of these! I'd even wager this airhead will mix up Great Danes and Weimaraners." Ferdinand is on his game—it takes him less than two seconds to identify the German shepherd, then the Doberman pinscher. He stumbles on the Dogo Argentino, which he wouldn't have put in the attack dog category, when there's a knock at the door.

"If that's Christine coming back to say good-bye, you're too late, old girl!" he said, turning up the TV. "You left me in a pickle and I'm not in the mood . . ." The person rings the doorbell. "I must be dreaming! People are beyond presumptuous. I really oughtta disconnect it. That damned bell is double trouble—I pay for the electricity so they can bug me . . ."

"Hello?" a man's voice calls out. "I'm sorry to bother you. Is anyone there? I'm your new neighbor."

Ferdinand sits up. *How dare he? I'd keep a low profile if I were him!*

"Is anyone there?"

Ferdinand stands and, via the peephole, learns who's responsible for his day of torture. *A man, that's something anyway—there won't be any high heels!* Maybe forty years old, brown hair, a relatively soft voice. He's wearing a green sweatshirt. The new neighbor doesn't seem too awful.

"Is anyone there? I just wanted to introduce myself. I just moved in upstairs, my name is Antoine and—"

"Let me stop you right there. I think I've had my fill of introductions. You can go back home. I've heard enough of you for today. You, your baby, your furniture! Good-bye, sir."

Ferdinand watches his crestfallen neighbor, shoulders slumped, head back to the stairs. The old man returns to his armchair. The door upstairs slams. With all this nonsense, Ferdinand missed the rest of the categories in "Four in a Row." Of course. It's his favorite part. Couldn't that damned neighbor have waited?

***

Ferdinand decides to go to bed early. Too bad for the weekly late-night variety show, but in any case it's always the same musical numbers, the same guests, the same jokes—and rarely funny for that matter. The kid stopped crying around 8:00 p.m. She must be sleeping now. Ferdinand resets his alarm. He has to recuperate. He turns out all the lights, and it takes him no more than five minutes to drift off and enjoy six hours of restorative sleep before the alarm goes off.

Beep. Beep. Beep.

Ferdinand feels fit as a fiddle. He goes into the living room, clears his wheeled serving cart, then sets down a dusty turntable that hasn't been used in over twenty years. He rummages through a chest and pulls out an LP—his favorite. He pushes the whole thing toward his bedroom.

He plugs in the device, positions the vinyl record, sets it turning, and lowers the needle. The device crackles, and all of a sudden, as if an orchestra had stormed Ferdinand's bedroom, the booming voice of Frank Sinatra—a.k.a. Ol' Blue Eyes—starts singing "Almost Like Being in Love." Ferdinand smiles. Time seems to have leapt backward by close to sixty-five years. He loves this song, especially the beginning. He turns up the volume all the way and puts the turntable on top of his wardrobe, inches from the ceiling. Dust bunnies flutter above him.

Ten, nine, eight . . . As he reaches five, he hears a baby begin to wail. Ferdinand sings along with Ol' Blue Eyes and puts his whole heart into it. "I could *swear* I was falling!" He knows all the words and keeps time by tapping his foot with the same enthusiasm as Fred Astaire in *Happy Feet*.

Overhead, a door opens. Heavy steps come to get the baby.

"It's three-oh-five in the morning, on the dot! Welcome, dear neighbors!" And Ferdinand starts singing even louder, "It's almost . . . like bein' . . . in . . . love!"

Chapter Fourteen

Popped His Cherry

For Ferdinand, that baby is the greatest of misfortunes. He despises, above all else, infants. For him, they are nothing but limitations, with the added bonus of utter ingratitude. They understand nothing, they cry, they always need something. You can never rest. And when they smile, they smile at strangers as much as at their parents. *Ingrates, away with you!* Furthermore, you're supposed to think they're cute, gifted . . . But a human being who drools, isn't capable of stringing three words together, and walks like a drunkard? No, Ferdinand cannot fake it!

Besides, he didn't want kids. It was his wife who got pregnant without consulting him. OK, they'd talked about it, but nothing had been decided. He'd always told Louise, "If you want a child, you look after it. I don't want it to change my routine. It's already gonna cost us an arm and a leg. I think I'll have to do overtime at the factory."

It's not that Ferdinand is a tightwad, but he's thrifty. With money and emotion. And children—unless you have twelve and put them to work—cost more than they bring in! His wife had taken a bookkeeping job for extra money and, a short time later, got pregnant.

Ferdinand had been in denial about the pregnancy. As if he didn't really believe something was going to come out of that belly—a belly that was indisputably expanding. He never wanted to prepare the nursery. He didn't attend the birth. And when he came home to discover it was a girl, he was disappointed. He even blamed his wife. She could call it whatever she wanted. Marion . . . What an idea, honestly!

Then, there were nothing but limitations: bottles, burping, diapers, baths, insomnia, shopping, laundry . . . continuously, day and night. Ferdinand didn't feel involved, but just seeing his wife bustle around so much made him tired. When he wasn't at the factory, he slept on the living room sofa to catch up on his rest. Sometimes he even avoided the house.

His wife's demeanor grew increasingly grim. She started to let herself go, like all women of a certain age—thirty years make themselves known. When he returned home after work, it was always the same scene: Louise would sulk at him, his daughter would cry at the sight of him, and at bedtime there'd be no fooling around. The beginning of the end. It's no surprise Marion didn't have a little brother.

The little girl grew up. She sat up in her bath, ate chunky purees, waddled like a duck, babbled in an incomprehensible language, had an imaginary best friend, played with dolls. Then there was the "why" stage, school, good grades, graduation. The first high school graduate in the Brun family.

**

Throughout all those years, Marion saw her parents argue daily. The plates flew from Louise as often as the insults. Her father ignored the verbal and physical attacks as best he could and was content to consider his wife crazy. The fights ended the same way every time: Louise hid in the bedroom in tears, while Ferdinand sat in the living room, a newspaper in his lap and the TV on in the background.

Marion doesn't remember sharing anything with her father, aside from her unusual stature. As a woman, her five-foot-eleven-inch height has always been an obstacle. She forgoes high heels, which might have been able to feminize her shape. It was difficult to find a man taller than she was, and one who wasn't intimidated by her shoulders.

Early on, Marion turned toward a career that would distance her from her parents: international diplomacy. It was hardly a surprise after spending years with parents consumed by arguing. At any rate, she'd left with the first guy who came along, a policeman she met at a nightclub. They'd danced to Chaka Khan's "Fate." She'd taken that as a sign and married him. Neither of the two families had been invited to the ceremony. Later she'd gotten pregnant with a boy, then had divorced amicably. When the divorce was final, she accepted a position abroad in London, then in Singapore, which wasn't a problem for her ex-husband, who was relieved by not having to be one of those new exemplary fathers, the ones who claim to be happy about getting joint custody. Visits during school vacations suited them all just fine.

Ferdinand has never understood how his daughter could ask for a divorce and abandon her husband, whom he certainly didn't hold dear. Marion doesn't hold it against Ferdinand. Defying all expectations, she's always been indulgent with her father, finding excuses for his absences, defending him against her mother.

***

When it was Ferdinand's turn to get a letter from Louise demanding a divorce, he'd at first thought it was a joke. A trick played very late, over the age of eighty, when he wasn't expecting it anymore, when he thought the worst was behind him, and the time to pay the piper had passed . . . or that the mailman had forgotten his address.

Chapter Fifteen

You Can Count Me Out

Ferdinand doesn't know why, but when his sorrows disappeared two weeks ago, just after the infamous nocturnal musical welcome, a pain formed in the lower half of his face. On the advice of his doctor, he's once again wearing his bandage and taking painkillers.

It's past noon, but with his jaw swaddled, the old man dreads mealtimes, when he inevitably bites off more than he can chew. He's resigned to swapping his usual rump steak for boiled ham, and macaroni for alphabet pasta. And he can now once again stomach things besides soup, even if he still has to eat with a spoon. It is a humiliation that feels like a foretaste of the retirement home . . . But what irritates Ferdinand the most is the pitcher of water presiding over the Formica table. The doctor was strict: no alcohol! Armed with his little spoon, Ferdinand is cautiously opening his mouth, when the doorbell rings. He freezes, then glances at the clock. It's 12:18. The spoon remains suspended an inch from his lips. Who would dare disturb him during lunch? *I'm not home.*

But there are two additional knocks. Ferdinand groans, steps into his slippers, and shuffles to the door. When he peers out the peephole to identify the lout, he sees no one. All that fuss for nothing . . . Ferdinand is still leaning against the door, looking through the peephole, when someone rings the bell again. What kind of joke is this? The old man violently yanks open the door. There, on the doormat, is a little girl, about ten. A puny thing, in overalls and a striped shirt. She doesn't have time to open her mouth before Ferdinand stops her cold.

"Don't bother exerting yourself, little one. I already have my calendar for the year. You're not too clever coming by after January."

He's closing the door, when a shoe gets in the way. Stunned, Ferdinand watches the little girl come inside and sit down in the kitchen.

"What are you doing? Get out of my house, kid. On the double!"

"Sorry, but your head looks like an Easter egg! If *I* had to commit suicide, I wouldn't throw myself under a bus. Too much risk of failure, don't you think?"

Ferdinand's jaw is about to drop, when the little girl continues. "I brought some licorice. I thought it could be dessert for us. I bet you don't have anything in your fridge."

She gets up, opens it, and her cursory inspection yields a "Bingo!" Ferdinand, speechless, watches as the girl strolls around his home. No one has set foot in his kitchen for years. No one!

"You're gonna have to do some serious cleaning before Mrs. Suarez visits you on Wednesday. Otherwise, you're finished!" concludes the little girl, sitting back down.

Enough is enough. Ferdinand finally manages to form some words. "Hold on. Who are *you*, first of all? And what are you doing in my kitchen? And nobody talks to me like that! No way—"

"I've come for lunch. I don't like the cafeteria. My name's Juliette. I'm going to call you Ferdinand, it'll be easier that way."

"I'm only going to repeat this once: you pack up your bag and get the hell out of here. Such insolence!"

"I thought you might need your medicine. Don't you? You forgot it at the pharmacy."

Juliette puts the plastic pharmacy bag on the table. "Good thing I'm here! So, what are we eating? I'm starving. Ham and macaroni? You have a fork anywhere? I'm not really into spoons. I leave that to my sister, Emma. She's one and a half. I think you've already met her, and my father, too. We just moved in upstairs, into the hairdresser's old apartment. Apparently she decided to leave because she was getting mean. I don't really get it."

Ferdinand remains silent. He slumps into his chair and points to the drawer in the china cabinet where the flatware is kept. In a slightly calmer voice, he tries again. "But you can't just turn up like this. I'm expecting company. You have to leave."

"Bah, if there's enough for two or three, there's enough for four! When are your guests arriving? Don't mind me, but school starts back up at one thirty, so I mustn't dawdle. Fine, I'll split it into two and you can redo it however you need to. You sure you don't want to start? I'm not very comfortable with you looking at me like that." She takes a bite. "Did you know they're saying you're a serial killer? And that you might have killed your wife? Where is your wife, Ferdinand?" the little girl inquires with her mouth full.

The old man shuts his eyes. This is just a bad dream. He's going to wake up, and everything will be like before. He reopens his eyes. It's 12:50 p.m., half the meal has disappeared, his stomach is crying out for food, and the little chatterbox with a vocabulary far beyond her years is still there.

"At least take some licorice. You're gonna pass out. I bought it with my lunch money." Juliette wipes her mouth on her sleeve and adds, "OK, I've gotta run now. I have to go back to the pharmacy to look for my sister's milk. You're welcome for the medicine. See you tomorrow at 12:15! I'll bring the bread and dessert."

The tsunami departs as quickly as it had come. Words like *Easter egg*, *serial killer*, and *licorice* remain in its wake. Everything spins around Ferdinand. The only thing he is certain of is that the next day at 12:15, he will not open up! The little girl had taken advantage of the element of surprise, a moment of weakness due to his accident. But the next day he will not be taken in. "Not by a child!" he rants while pounding his fist into the table. In a state of advanced hypoglycemia, he seizes the box of licorice and gulps down a piece. The rest of the box follows.

Chapter Sixteen
Fit for the Loony Bin

Ferdinand is preoccupied. He's forgotten something but no longer knows what. That worries him. Ferdinand is a hypochondriac. This mustn't be Alzheimer's . . . Anything but that! Losing his mind would be the worst thing he could imagine. He's already going deaf . . . He has to keep all his wits. And his legs, too. Otherwise he won't be able to climb the thirteen steps up to his apartment. And he'll have to move. Probably to the retirement home. Oh, no, anything but the retirement home.

Furthermore, he's waiting for the silly old goose and her pathetic inspection. He's ready to welcome her as required. Maybe *ready* isn't the right word. Mrs. Suarez is coming at 4:00 p.m. and *nothing* is ready. He has to tidy up, take out the trash, go shopping, clean, take a bath, even wash his hair. His lair is a chaotic dump. The old lady will faint just at the smell: between the trash cans, the dust, the odor of grease and mothballs—even he recognizes it doesn't smell like roses. Then again, if she croaks, that would solve all his problems! Well, unless she kicks the bucket in his house. Then they'd really take him for a serial killer.

It's 11:55. He'll never be ready . . . Barring a miracle!

Chapter Seventeen

To Beat the Band

On Tuesday, at 12:15 on the dot, Juliette appears at the door.

"Ferdinand, it's me, Juliette. Open up! I know you're there. I saw you skulk back from the butcher hugging the walls. I've brought bread!"

Behind his door, Ferdinand nods. *She can stick her bread where the sun don't shine. Besides, I still have some left over, which will do nicely.*

The little girl rings again. "If you don't let me in, I'll keep ringing until 1:15. Being an only child for so long has taught me patience. Open up! I have something for you . . ."

Ferdinand won't be taken in by this little manipulator. He's intrigued, but it's out of the question for her to invite herself over for lunch every day. He values his peace and quiet. Anyway, he's no cook, much less a nanny. And today he doesn't have time for this childishness; he has other things to worry about, namely Mrs. Suarez's visit. However, as might be gathered from his stomach's noises, he can't help but salivate when thinking about the previous day's melt-in-your-mouth sweets.

A glance at the empty licorice box, and he risks asking through the door, "What have you brought that's so extraordinary I'm going to let you in? Licorice? Because if it's that, I'm not the least bit interested. I still have plenty. And I don't have time to eat today, let alone babysit. For free, no less!"

"Two things. Firstly, I bet there's nothing left in yesterday's box. So, I bought a dessert. I changed it up. I got candied chestnuts. Secondly, I brought something else. Isn't Mrs. Suarez coming tomorrow?"

Why yes! The silly old goose isn't coming until tomorrow. The inspection is on Wednesday, and today is only Tuesday. Ferdinand sighs with relief. He has more time. How could he have been mistaken? And how does the little girl know?

"Listen, Little Miss Know-It-All. Yes, Mrs. Suarez is coming tomorrow, but that's none of your beeswax! And for your information, the licorices weren't even that good. You can go home now and say hello to your father for me!"

Juliette remains unruffled. "I thought that apart from the white vinegar you put in your dressings you must not have much to scrub your apartment with. So I got—if you're interested, of course—a floor cleaner, a bathroom and kitchen cleaner, a hard water treatment, a window cleaner, two sponges, three rags, and a mop. We have quite the supply at home. Our housekeeper is afraid of running out."

The door opens like magic. *"Open sesame"* wouldn't have been more effective. Pretending to be unmoved, Ferdinand carries on. "I was waiting for you before starting lunch, little one. It's ready. Hurry up, it'll get cold. Tell me, when you say window cleaner, do you think it's worth doing the windows for Mrs. Suarez? It rained all week—that cleans them, doesn't it?"

Juliette sits in the same blue Formica chair from the previous day, across from Ferdinand.

"I don't know if you've noticed," she says, pointing to the window, "but Mrs. Suarez does her windows every Saturday before hosting her friends. When I came yesterday, I didn't dare say anything, but your windows are so dirty you'd think it's night outside. Mrs. Suarez might wince at that even if the rest of the apartment is spotless. You'll also have to clean your fridge," she says as she puts a plastic bag inside. "She has to make sure you're feeding yourself, so I brought you some eggs and green beans and pickles. That'll be much better than moldy cheese and rancid butter. Will you throw them out yourself, or should I do it now?" Without waiting for a reply, she seizes the two biological weapons and dumps them into the trash bag.

Ferdinand isn't hungry anymore with all this talk of housework. The last time he cleaned was so long ago that it depresses him thinking about scrubbing, scouring, washing, dusting . . . Taking out the trash already takes him days. Days of dithering before deciding to do it, forced by the nauseating stench emanating from the bag and filling the kitchen. To find out when Ferdinand has thrown out a bag of garbage, you only have to observe his kitchen window—when it's open, it's because he's finally decided to do it, just before the bugs arrive. In his entire life he's only done housework maybe twice, and he doesn't have any concrete memory of it. He's nearing the point of telling himself it wouldn't be so bad at a retirement home. At least he wouldn't have to worry about cleaning, laundry, or meals. Lost in thought, he pushes his plate away and rummages in the plastic bag that Juliette put in the fridge, looking for chestnuts.

Juliette asks, "You want another spoon of macaroni or can I finish it off?"

"You don't say 'spoon.' You say 'spoonful.' Haven't your parents taught you anything?"

"My mother is dead. My father works a lot. He's a landscape designer, specializing in sustainable development."

"Well, good. So you go to school. What grade are you in?"

"Fifth."

"Fifth? You're quite the chatterbox for your age."

"That's what the teacher says, too. Now it's my turn to ask questions. Why are you all alone? Is your wife dead?"

"What makes you think I have a wife?"

"You seem like somebody who thinks his life is over. You remind me of those old people who think that each passing day isn't worth living, that they'd be better off dead because they'll never know happiness again. I have a book about it. It's called *Old Age, Depression, and Addiction*."

"Should you be reading things like that? You've got a screw loose, my dear, I'm telling you."

"It was to better understand my grandmother. She was very sad when her man-friend died. What are *you* reading? Thrillers, I bet. OK, so then, what happened to your wife?"

"I don't like to talk about it. I get angry. I have regrets. I shouldn't have done certain things. But now it's too late. And now it's time to leave, Juliette. We'll discuss literature another time."

The moment the words leave his mouth, Ferdinand wants them back. He doesn't want her to take them as an invitation to drop by every day for lunch—he has other things to deal with.

"OK. I'm off. By the way, do you know how to use the things I brought you?"

Ferdinand feigns indignation. Juliette continues. "In addition to the toilets, don't forget to wipe the floor. It's sticky—my sneakers are sticking to the parquet and a strip just got torn up. It's not like that in people's houses, normally."

He finally—thankfully—closes the door on Juliette, all while calculating how long he can postpone the drudgery of housework. He decides to take a nap while listening to his favorite radio program, *True Crime*. Might as well get the pleasures in before the chores. Though no matter how much he does and redoes the calculation, he arrives at the same result: he's behind. And he's going to have to make compromises. Certainly on the windows, and toilets, too. For the straightening up, he'll find a closet in which to toss everything he hasn't found a place for in two years. As for the rest, it's bad. Up the creek, even.

Oh, well, since he's screwed anyway, Ferdinand settles into his armchair, puts his feet up, pulls the blanket over him, and awaits the beginning of his program, eyelids already heavy. It can all wait until tomorrow, and it'll be for the best: the silly old goose isn't the queen of England! A little sleight of hand, and she'll be completely hoodwinked.

Chapter Eighteen

Up the Wall

Only three hours separate Ferdinand from Mrs. Suarez's inspection, and he still hasn't touched the cleaning products. The silly old goose has just left him a letter indicating she's moved the inspection up by a day: she'll be showing up today, Tuesday, at 6:00 p.m.

It was while barely woken up from his postlunch nap and still unsteady that Ferdinand discovered a letter slipped under his door. Since then his heart has been racing.

What an old bag that concierge is! Ideally, Mrs. Suarez gets held up with something else this afternoon. Ferdinand reflects for a few minutes. *I think I've found something to distract her for a couple hours.*

One problem persists, however. Even if Mrs. Suarez doesn't come until Wednesday, as planned, Ferdinand still has to tackle the cursed housework, and soon. A saying surfaces in his memory, one his old supervisors used to use every time Ferdinand made a suggestion: "We can't all be good at everything." A way of sending him packing and asking him to concentrate on his own work instead of his neighbor's. And it's true that Ferdinand's thing, his forte, is . . . what is it, anyway? One thing is certain: it's not housework! Then again, a woman, more precisely a cleaning woman, would know how to solve the problem. But where to find such an expert on short notice?

Ferdinand sees two options—either ask Juliette for their housekeeper's contact info, or ask one of the neighbor ladies for her housekeeper's contact info. But Ferdinand doesn't fancy letting Juliette know he wasn't able to do his housework. He had the time—taking into account the diversion he's planning—and he had the products. But neither the desire nor the courage. As for the second option, he'd have to find a neighbor lady who wouldn't say anything to Mrs. Suarez, and that's mission impossible. Ferdinand is at an impasse. Or he could call an agency and pray they send someone competent. But it's likely all the good ones are taken. The clock is ticking. Ferdinand decides to set up Mrs. Suarez's diversion.

His trap set, Ferdinand is climbing back up the stairs when he hears the door slam on the second floor. Darn, it's the old bat Mrs. Claudel. He doesn't want to cross paths with her, not now. She's going to ask him how he's been doing since Daisy. Back against the wall, he risks a peek. Oh, no, she's carrying glass bottles. She's going to ruin everything if she goes in the trash area.

Shoot! Ferdinand has no choice: he has to detain her, otherwise, it's the retirement home for sure! He climbs the last few steps and calls out, "Hello, ma'am. I'd like to have a word with you, if you don't mind. It's important and extremely urgent."

"Of course, Mr. Brun. What is it?" she asks in surprise.

"Since my dog died, there are too many memories at home. It would be easier for me to say good-bye if I had some help to put her things away."

"I was just about to go to church—I'm organizing guided tours there—but tomorrow afternoon I can give you a hand. I understand this isn't exactly easy."

"That's very kind of you, but I was thinking more along the lines of your housekeeper. You do have one, don't you?"

Beatrice nods.

"Could you ask her to do me a favor? The sooner the better."

"If it's that urgent, you should call her right now."

Beatrice gets her keys out of her purse and motions for Ferdinand to follow her. A few steps into the entryway, he's dazzled by the brightness and beauty of the place. How can an apartment identical to his own, and with the same exposure, be so different? Magnificent, even. How can he be bathed in sunlight at 3:50 p.m.? Everything is in perfect order and sparkling clean. It's like being in a mansion. The walls are papered in a discreet English pattern, with beautiful moldings and millwork. The chandeliers and chevron-patterned parquet floor give the impression of a ballroom. The timeless family heirloom furniture is ornamented with finely gilded handles. On the walls are numerous oil paintings, probably paying homage to illustrious family members. Above the old mantel hangs a masterpiece—the portrait of a marshal of the Empire, surely an illustrious member of the Claudel family.

Most impressive, however, is the library that occupies the entire length of the dining room wall. The wood is magnificent, the finish delicate. The wide shelves hold hundreds of old books, arranged by publisher, whose gilded bindings match the amber color of the wood. Ferdinand doesn't know much about art, literature, or even décor, but wood, yes: the beauty of the parquet, the baseboards, and the library greatly impresses him and informs him of his host's noble birth.

"Mr. Brun? Are you still with me? I'm on the phone with Katia, my housekeeper. She can come tomorrow morning at nine o'clock, if you wish. It was the time reserved for me, but I'll make do with the dust for a few extra days, don't worry about it."

Mess? Dust? Here?

"Mr. Brun? Does that work for you?"

"Yes, it's perfect. Thank you so much for your help, ma'am . . ."

"Claudel, Beatrice Claudel! All right, let's go, I'm frightfully late."

Ferdinand reaches the landing ahead of Beatrice, but stops on his doorstep, searching for his keys. Beatrice, in a hurry as usual, waves one last time before heading down the stairs. *OK, she's gone.* It's out of the question for her to see the inside of *his* apartment. After what he saw, Ferdinand will never dare let her enter his place.

In any case, his cleaning problem is resolved: tomorrow an expert on dusting and tidying will come take care of his apartment.

But something has been nagging at him since he thought to call a housekeeper and even more since visiting with his neighbor. How much does a cleaning lady, one used to polishing up rich peoples' houses, cost? That's as far as his thinking makes it, when a fire engine siren blares from the courtyard.

Damn! I didn't have time to call the fire department . . . Well, they're already here, that's the main thing. I hope my diversion will soon be under control and won't make the front page tomorrow . . .

***

From his window, Ferdinand takes in the sight of firemen. After more than an hour and a half of battling a fire at the back of the courtyard, they extract a metal box, enveloped in flames, from the trash area and spray it with their fire hose to the point of inundating Mrs. Suarez's lovely flower boxes. All the while, she bosses everyone around.

Ferdinand looks at the clock. 6:12 p.m. The silly old goose won't come today for her inspection! He's saved.

***

At that moment, the concierge looks up and sees the old man watching her. She waves at him, murmuring to herself, "Just you wait, you old geezer!"

Chapter Nineteen

Having a Cow

As usual on Wednesday evenings, the TV lineup is depressing. No proper films, just reruns of American shows whose plots cater to the lowest common denominator. All that to push people into going to the cinema. Ferdinand, however, has opted for *CSI*—it'll be fine playing in the background. The day could have been joyful—Mrs. Suarez's inspection went well—but he's preoccupied. He spent the evening trying to call his daughter to tell her about the concierge's visit, before the silly old goose could rewrite history, but the telephone just rang and rang.

Marion is one of those unbearable people who never answer their phone. Ferdinand has come to terms with it over the years, but in this case, it's really important. After more than twenty-five fruitless attempts, he's frustrated. What if there's an emergency? How could he let her know? He even tries her cell phone. What's worse is that it doesn't ring and doesn't offer to let him leave a voice mail. Marion will give him her usual excuse: "I probably ran out of battery." Couldn't she be a bit responsible for once? To think, he'd almost considered apologizing for their last conversation. There's no risk of that occurring to him again for a while . . .

This isn't the first time Marion's been unreachable, but it's the first time it's put him in this state. Something's eating at him. And he can't swallow a bite except for a few spoonfuls of tasteless cream-of-potato soup. He was doing better for several days, but once again he's feeling deep sadness. An even greater loneliness. Like a patient in relapse. And nobody seems to care. He hides behind his anger, but he knows his malaise doesn't really have anything to do with Marion. He's used to his perfunctory relationship with his daughter.

He's lacking something else. Juliette . . . He sighs, that's what's bothering him. She hasn't come around. Although she didn't say she'd come back, Ferdinand expected her for lunch. Hoped? No, let's not get carried away . . . But somehow or other, the little girl is rather good company. A bit like Daisy, but in her own way. Badly brought up, saying anything that comes into her head, no respect for her elders. Entertaining, though, with her impertinent questions and improbable reading. He'll find out what happened tomorrow, at least, if she comes back, and he'll tell her about Mrs. Suarez's visit.

Ferdinand is dozing when a dull thud, like pounding on a thick pane of glass, makes him jump. He opens his eyes. Something is moving on the balcony, right in front of him. A little shadow. It looks like . . . the slight figure of a child. Juliette! She's motioning on the balcony and banging on the glass. The old man rubs his eyes. Is he dreaming or is the little girl really there waving at him? *She really does have bats in her belfry!* He goes to let her in.

"How could you jump down from the third floor? Are you nuts? You could have gotten yourself killed! And it's freezing out there. Get inside, quick!" She steps inside as he shuffles back to his armchair.

"I didn't jump. I'm not crazy, you know . . . I took out the trash and then I thought I'd come see you. I didn't want to ring the bell in case you were sleeping, so I climbed up the rose trellises. One floor is easy. Besides, I hope you close your shutters at night. Anybody could walk right in, if you ask me."

"You didn't want to wake me up by ringing, but you bang like a madwoman on my clean windows? You don't think that disturbed me even more? And what are you doing here at this hour? Shouldn't a little girl of . . . of your age be in bed at nine thirty-five? What's your father going to say when he realizes you haven't come back from the trash area?"

"Tonight he's working on a new building site. Katia, our housekeeper, is babysitting us. She fell asleep in front of the TV. You exhausted her yesterday. I've never seen her miss an episode of *CSI.*"

Juliette sits down on the sofa and wraps herself in the blanket.

"You must have noticed I couldn't come today. It's Wednesday and on Wednesday I have lunch with Papa since there's no school.

So how did Mrs. Suarez's inspection go? It looks like our house-keeper did a fabulous job. It still smells clean."

"Hey, Miss Bold-as-Brass, I didn't call your housekeeper. I had your cleaning stuff and it was a piece of cake. I—"

"Don't lie, Ferdinand. Katia told me everything. She spoke of certain places, like behind the fridge . . . She'd never seen that! Mrs. Claudel recommended her housekeeper to us when we moved in. So, what did Mrs. Suarez say to so much cleanliness? Did she purse her lips like she does when she's upset at having nothing to complain about?"

"You know her well, I'd say. Yes, Mrs. Suarez remained true to form. A real little gestapo captain."

Ferdinand gets up out of his armchair and paces in front of Juliette, in a pale imitation of the concierge.

"She did her duty, in silence, frowning, lips pursed. She came in, peeked in every room, opened every cupboard, checked the cleaning products under the sink, inspected the windows, examined the balcony, unscrewed the liquid-hand-soap bottle, scrutinized the sponges, picked up the phone receiver, glanced at the trash can, and lifted up the bedspread to see if the sheets were clean. She smirked when she found a bit of dust on top of the baseboards. She also ordered me to remove the plastic bag from the fridge, lest the green beans go bad."

"Oh, yes, I should have thought of that . . ."

"But ultimately, I think it went well. I even took a bath and put on cologne. The president of the republic wouldn't have been treated better! Besides, I was a bit tricksy: I offered her coffee. She didn't even deign to respond, she just made another face like 'coffee from that old machine with its gym-sock filters?' She's coming back next month. I'm not going to put up with these inspections forever. I'm not a kid! I called Marion to stop this charade, but she's not answering on purpose. Say, you want to munch on something? I might have some pretzels," says Ferdinand, opening the door on the sideboard.

"I'd prefer more pickles, if there are any left."

The old man gets the jar and sits back down in his armchair.

"I'm glad everything went well with Mrs. Suarez. Wasn't she surprised not to find any alcohol here?"

"Why do you say that? What do you know about it? Did your housekeeper tell you something? I'm not an alcoholic. So it stands to reason there isn't a drop of alcohol in the house. What are you insinuating?"

"Calm down, Ferdinand, I'm not insinuating anything. I'm just saying it's shady that there's no wine, or aperitif, or liqueur. But you have aperitif glasses and snifters. That implies a stash."

"Nonsense, Juliette! You really have an overactive imagination for your age."

"And Mrs. Suarez didn't say anything about your . . . straight razor? That's what it's called, right? Basically, your old razor's a little scary. Remember, she's charged with verifying that you don't want to hurt yourself or others."

"How can you say such things? Where do you get ideas like that?"

"In one of the books I borrowed from you—your collection of Pierre Bellemare's *Extraordinary Stories*."

"You borrowed a book from me? When? Aren't you ashamed to help yourself like that?"

"Last time. Anyhow, sorry, your reading simply will not do. And if Mrs. Suarez hasn't said anything yet, it's because she didn't see you only have stories about murders, corrupt police officers, and the war."

"That's not all I have. I also have a dictionary and—"

Juliette concluded, "Oh, yes, it's true, you also have books about dogs. But they're all about guard and attack dogs. That's not going to improve Mrs. Suarez's image of you. A serial killer—remember?"

"I couldn't care less! The silly old goose can go to hell. I'm not going to buy books to please her. I don't read anymore anyway, so there's no point. Time doesn't pass any quicker and I don't have anybody to talk about it with after."

"I can help make your library presentable. I'll bring you my father's horticulture books, for example. But I doubt gardening books would interest you," says Juliette, looking around. "You don't have any plants. Not even on the balcony. What a shame."

"Concentrate, will you? OK, bring your father's books. So, if I may summarize, my second inspection runs the risk of turning sour because of a razor and alcohol? I'll make sure to buy all of that. But do you know how much more a modern razor costs? The blades especially—they're thirty euros for a package of five!

And alcohol isn't cheap, either. As for the plants, you can forget it. That's for women."

"Tell that to my father and you'll get an earful!" retorts Juliette, smiling.

"What I mean is it's not *at all* my thing. I'm more Roundup ready, you see. Wherever I pass by, everything passes away. It was my wife who had the green thumb."

"Where is your wife?"

"We separated years ago. She left me. There. Now you know everything."

"That's all?"

"Don't get offended, but I won't tell you any more. And why are you interested in the life of an old gentleman like myself anyway? A girl of your age has nothing better to do?"

"Let's just say I'm different. A little precocious, it would seem," Juliette says as she grabs her umpteenth pickle. "Since I know things that don't interest the girls and boys my age, they call me 'the brain.' They think I'm haughty because I use words longer than two syllables. I don't do it on purpose, I'm just like that. What I like to do is garden, play Scrabble or *Questions for a Champion*, read, people-watch, eat cake . . . Maybe that's why I prefer being with older people. They say you become an adult when you realize you have to die one day. For me, that was at age six when I lost my paternal grandfather. A stupid bicycle accident. It was a shock for me. I adored my Pappy."

"Is that why you come see me?"

"Don't get offended, but you're polar opposites. I started visiting you because you were the only grandpa in the complex, and I wanted to avoid the cafeteria at school. Now I like you. You make me laugh and I need that. The past year hasn't been fun for me. My mama . . . no one could do anything. She was an extraordinary woman. Very beautiful and very intelligent, too. She was a special correspondent. She wasn't at home much. One day, she was taken to the hospital. She'd been shot in the arm while covering a story. They kept her under observation. Then her condition deteriorated. They found out afterward that she'd caught an infection. I miss Mama enormously, but I'm trying not to think about her too much. I just want to keep my promise: work hard at school and be nice to Papa and Emma. That's all."

"I'm sorry about your mama. Your story's very sad."

"What about you, Ferdinand? Why are you all alone?"

"Well, my story is everyone's story. My wife, she was sick of me, I think. Sick of my absences, our shouting matches. One day, when I came back after a few weeks away, she'd made her decision. I hadn't seen it coming. She'd found my replacement. The mailman! Can you imagine? She took the first guy to come along. And an Italian, no less! To think that bastard was coming by every day to chitchat with her. One day, I even had the bright idea of inviting him in for coffee. Me, a cuckold! I'll never accept it. I even wanted her to die. They went off to the south of France and I assume they had a lousy life together."

Ferdinand pauses. It costs him to trust anybody—more than he imagines.

"Well, to make a long story short, a few months ago she did die. She fell getting out of the bathtub. I found out about it from Marion. It hit me pretty hard. Not so much her death, but everything it signified. Deep down, I always thought she'd come back, that she'd say, 'I'm sorry, I was wrong, I can't live without you.' But no. She was never sorry, apparently. You're going to say I'm naïve. You see, from my entire life there's nothing but failures, regrets. A failed marriage, a daughter who doesn't really love me and who fled to the other side of the world, a grandson I've seen a total of eight times . . . My only reason for living was Daisy. Without really knowing it, I was living for her. It's funny, it was my wife who gave her to me for our last Christmas. Sometimes I wonder if she'd already planned to leave me. There. Now you really know everything."

"That's why you wanted to die? You picked the bus so you could go the way Daisy did?"

"I hadn't considered that I'd picked the bus to go like Daisy, run over. Maybe, after all . . . Well, how about we talk about something a little happier? Then you go on home before your nanny wakes up. What did you learn in school this week?"

"I learned something rather interesting, but it's not necessarily happier. We discussed the emergency actions to take in the event of a gas leak. It's part of the new lifesaving techniques being tested at my school. I've already learned CPR."

"I never did learn that. Certainly not at school. Is it easy to do?"

"With chest compressions there is still a risk of breaking ribs. But it's better to have a few broken bones and stay alive, in my opinion. I can teach you, if you want."

"Pff . . . At my age? It's not worth it. And to save who?"

"Me! If one day you turn on the gas and have regrets," says Juliette, smiling.

"Stop that nonsense, little one. Go on home now."

Ferdinand accompanies Juliette to the door.

"I was just wondering, which is your favorite Pierre Bellemare story?"

"The one with the black-eyed garbage chute. It scares your pants off. Ever since reading it, I haven't dared use the one on the landing."

Chapter Twenty
Pardon?

It's extraordinary how people can take a smile for an invitation to chat. As Ferdinand returns home from the Franprix supermarket, laden with pickles, ham, and macaroni for lunch, he suddenly finds himself nose to nose with Mrs. Claudel exiting her apartment. He faintly produces the beginnings of an almost friendly smile, then turns his back to insert his keys in the lock when his neighbor says in her strident voice, "Hello there, Mr. Brun. How did you like Katia? Was she able to put the affairs of your late canine in order?"

Ferdinand swallows wrong and coughs a little before managing to utter a few words. "Uh . . . yes. You could say she was very effective. Anyway, I think I should—"

"I'm sorry to be impolite but I've got to run, Mr. Brun. My fitness class starts in fifteen minutes and I'm none too fast. However,

I'd be delighted to hear more about Katia's prowess. Come over for coffee today. But no niceties. Don't bring flowers or chocolates. I'll say toodle-oo, now, Mr. Brun. See you at two o'clock."

Ferdinand doesn't have time to decline as his neighbor disappears down the stairs, without waiting for a response. As though it's obvious Ferdinand is available, as though it's obvious he drinks coffee, as though it's obvious he feels like skipping his favorite radio program.

The old man has no choice: he's going to have to bite the bullet for half an hour in exchange for the assistance Mrs. Claudel provided. It's the least he can do.

The least he can do? Really, she didn't make any unreasonable effort—she made a phone call! Ferdinand isn't going to start compromising. Since his accident, the neighbor ladies have rushed—wittingly and unwittingly—into his life. First Juliette, and now Mrs. Claudel. He must face facts: he doesn't scare anyone anymore and especially not those two. Just look at how they destabilize him and come back for more like a karate match. If Juliette has already racked up the equivalent of eight points (against Ferdinand's zero), Mrs. Claudel achieved *ippon* in thirty seconds! No. Ferdinand must pull himself together. Regain the advantage. No one changes at his age. Let alone for the better.

In any case, Ferdinand has been intrigued since setting foot inside the old lady's apartment. All the more so since—as far as he can see through the peephole—Beatrice Claudel seems to have very interesting days. Much more interesting than his own. The invitation is a chance to verify whether his hypotheses about his neighbor's activities are correct.

Chapter Twenty-One

Great Caesar's Ghost

The clock in Ferdinand's kitchen says 2:05. He's standing on his neighbor's doormat, wondering if there's still time to retreat, when the door swings wide open.

"Come on in, Mr. Brun," Beatrice says. "Let me take your coat. Never fear, it's not cold in here. But do my eyes deceive me? Chocolates?"

"Uh, no, they're licorice. I know you asked me not to bring anything, but I think that's what you do when you're invited over. I'm not really sure anymore . . ."

"Oh, but you didn't have to! You've positively splurged! And I love licorice. This makes me very happy. Thank you so much, Mr. Brun. Please sit down. Do you take sugar in your coffee?" Beatrice pushes a steaming cup toward him.

"Um, yes, please. Your apartment is really quite lovely. Very different from mine."

"We bought it off-plan in 1957. I must still have the architect's drawing somewhere."

Beatrice takes something that isn't far off from a papyrus scroll out of a drawer.

"The paper's a bit yellow and the lines practically erased, but you can see the place's potential, can't you? What's funny is we initially chose your apartment, because you have the sun longer. But there was a mix-up during the allocation and in the end your in-laws got it. We didn't want to make a fuss, so we kept this one and had some work done before moving in. I haven't left it since, except for vacation or to go to my second home in Dinard. I enjoy it very much. These walls watched my four children grow up—it really was a happy home. I have wonderful memories here. Today, the apartment is much too large for me all alone. But, well, I'm rarely around. I'm very busy between my activities with the parish, the gym, my book club, going out to the theater or the movies, and the bridge club. Do you play bridge, Mr. Brun?"

"Uh, it's been so long I wouldn't be able to remember the rules."

"What marvelous news! A bridge player! I host a party every two weeks. I'll expect you at the next one. It's Tuesday night. And don't worry about the rules: we always go over them before every game, since we're all getting on in years. Would you like another cup? I always have a second."

"Um, yes, your coffee is very good."

"Since I get a lot of visitors—my grandchildren mostly—it's in my best interest to have decent coffee. On the other hand, you'll forgive me for not offering you a cigar, as I'd prefer the smell of tobacco not permeate the living room. My great-grandson is coming shortly."

"No problem, I don't smoke cigars anyhow. What made you think otherwise?"

"I thought I'd smelled cigar smoke in the stairwell behind you."

"Oh, yes . . . yes! To tell you the truth, I hate the smell of cigars, and pipe smoke even more, but I sometimes light one, to make me look interesting, I suppose."

"Why not! I'll let you have a second helping of licorice, Mr. Brun. I'm putting three aside for my great-grandson. Look, these are pictures of my grandchildren in the digital frame. They're not in order, but they give you an idea. They grow up so fast. There, that's me at the seaside, with them. Now I have to put on a wet suit to go swimming. As I get older, I find the sea colder than before."

"So many people! Who's the young woman next to you? She looks like the journalist Claire Chazal."

"One of my daughters-in-law. Why?"

"No reason. She's a beautiful woman, Claire Chazal—blond, elegant. Definitely my type. And who's the lady who looks like you, in that picture in the black frame on the sideboard?"

"My sister. She's just left us. I'm still quite grieved by her loss. We used to see each other every day. It's even harder than my poor husband's death, because at the time, with four children, I didn't have any choice but to go on. *The show must go on*, as the young-sters say," adds Beatrice in a thick British accent.

"I'm sorry. I didn't mean to stir up painful memories."

"My sister was an old lady, like me, and she was lucky enough not to be sick. You prepare yourself for that fateful day, but you can't help being sad when it arrives. That's life. And she had been less physically fit for a few years. She went in her sleep, at the age of eighty-nine. I like to think she went dreaming. 'A good death,' according to her grandchildren. She had thirty-four of them, you know."

"Thirty-four grandchildren! But how many children did she have?"

"Eight. I can't even tell you how many people that makes at family reunions. Next to her, I have a tiny little family, and it's already complicated to see everybody. Of course, you can't keep some of them from leaving to go live abroad—it would be selfish and unfair. Me, I've already lived my life, and fully. But it's always a blow to my morale to learn when one is moving away. It might be the last time I see them. For them, two years isn't so long. For me, every week is a gift. Fortunately we have Skype, Facebook, iPhones, and tablets, so I get news from them regularly. But it's not the same."

"What did you say? *Skip*? Like the laundry detergent? Never heard of it."

"No, *Skype*, with a *Y*. Like the sky. It's for telephoning every-where in the world with the computer. It's free. And it's very practical because there's video. You can see each other, and very well at that!"

"Sounds a bit like *Total Recall* with Arnold Schwarzenegger, when he made a call with a video intercom."

"Huh, I don't know that film. And I'm not too fond of the former California governor . . ."

"He's better known for his movies and his past work as a bodybuilder than for his political activities, anyway. But it's true that it made quite a stir in France when he outlawed the sale of foie gras in California."

"I'm enjoying your company, Mr. Brun. You're so refreshing. I won't deny it's more difficult for me to have a nice time with people my age. I won't insult you by saying '*our* age,' Mr. Brun," jokes the nonagenarian. "But barely a week goes by anymore without an invitation to a funeral or learning one of my friends has Parkinson's, Alzheimer's, or cancer. Just this morning I learned my sister-in-law isn't doing well. They found something. I'm keeping faith, but it's hard when you see your loved ones, even very young, taken before you. The secret to not sinking into despair is to learn to live with it and accept that death is part of life. 'Growing old means seeing others die.' I don't know anymore who said that, but I find it very apt. Don't you think, Mr. Brun?"

Beatrice continues without giving Ferdinand a chance to respond.

"And it's essential, of course, to find stimulating occupations so as not to end up with a stunted brain. Or infantilized by our own children. I'm outraged to see how some people—not mine, fortunately—behave: they order children's portions on our behalf in restaurants, or tell us 'never mind' as soon as we mishear something at the table. It's true, isn't it? All right, I'll stop bothering you. I invited you over to talk about Katia and then I bore you stiff with family stories. So how did the big spring cleaning go?"

"Very well. I wanted to thank you, Mrs. Claudel, for your help. Without you, and Katia, of course, I wouldn't have managed. I think I'll ask her for help with the housework on a more regular basis, if that doesn't bother you . . ."

"Not in the slightest, Mr. Brun. I know she's already extremely busy, even on the weekends, but she'll find a slot for you, I'm sure of it. Now, what about you? I don't mean to be nosy, but you've been living in the apartment across the way for two years, and we've spoken to each other three times at most. All I know about you is that it was your in-laws' apartment. Do you have children?"

"I have a daughter and a grandson. That's all. And they both live in Singapore, so we don't see each other often, unlike you and your family." Then, under the influence of panic, Ferdinand hears himself say, "So, what happened to your sister-in-law? Maybe I can do something?" Avoiding talking about his wife causes him to say anything.

"My sister-in-law is the last person really close to me I have left. Close to my age, I mean. Even though she's ninety years old and has all her wits, she's entering a retirement home because she's going blind. That reminds me of my mother. She also lost her sight suddenly. A problem with the optic nerve. She could only see like a horse with blinders on. The doctors had said it could wait until after vacation. And then at the beginning of August, curtains! She couldn't see a thing anymore except blue. Who knows why? With my sister, they made her move to an apartment close to us, so we could take care of her. But a few months after her move, she left us. Grief took her away: she could no longer remember her children's faces, or those of her grandchildren. She would tell me I was so beautiful, but she couldn't see my features anymore, my smiles . . . It pains me to think back on it. Oh, I don't know what you're doing to me, I'm all nostalgic. Usually I'm much more cheerful. I'm ashamed to have invited you over to tell you my sorrows."

"It's nothing. We all have our moments of weakness. You just heard about your sister-in-law, it's still fresh."

"Oh my goodness! We've been chitchatting away, and it's already four o'clock! I have to pick up my great-grandson at school. His parents are on a business trip, so he's sleeping here tonight. I always tell them they work too much. It wasn't like that back in our day, was it?"

"I don't know about you, but the factory was intense. What was your profession, Mrs. Claudel?"

"I have a law degree. I'm very proud to say I was the first woman admitted to the bar. Unfortunately, life made it so I could never practice. My husband's death, the children to raise, you know . . . I'll bore you another time with my old lady tales. I'm counting on you for our bridge party in two weeks. But we'll run into each other again before then. I'm so happy you made the first move . . . Ferdinand. I feel we have a lot in common. It was a shame to live so close and never exchange more than five words, don't you think? I'll see you out. Thanks again for the licorice. My great-grandson will have a feast. I'll tell him it comes from the nice neighbor."

As the door shuts behind him, Ferdinand can't help but smile and repeat Mrs. Claudel's last words. "Nice neighbor." It's the first time those words have been used to describe him! If only Marion could hear that. And if only Mrs. Claudel could be the one reporting to Marion rather than that silly old goose Mrs. Suarez. The best would be for the concierge to disappear from view, permanently, a bit like that horrible story about sudden blindness that had bowled him over.

Chapter Twenty-Two

Waiting for Godot

Ferdinand took offense at first, but now he's uneasy. Juliette hasn't come yet today, a Thursday. What if something has happened to her? It's bound to be serious, otherwise she would have let him know.

But Juliette hasn't shown up, not for lunch, nor after school. Ferdinand would like her to come, that's all. So, after *Questions for a Champion*, he takes a deep breath and goes to ring at her door. A man around forty years old opens it—his face is familiar.

"Yes, what is it? Can I help you? Hang on . . . who are you?"

Damn . . . Juliette's father! Ferdinand had nearly forgotten he'd been cold with him. Juliette has little in common with her unbearable little sister and her father, who thinks himself more courteous than everyone else, greeting his neighbors from day one. *If he could have given me a few more days, I might have welcomed him differently, but right then, with the noise from the move, the forced exile to the church, the crying baby, and fatigue on top of it all, it was too much!*

This is what Ferdinand tries to explain to Antoine, who is horrified by the incoherence of the old man's remarks. When Ferdinand eventually lets slip that he wants to know how Juliette is doing, because she didn't come over today, and that he'd bought her caramels, Antoine can't grasp the friendly, innocent nature of the situation.

"Get away from my home this minute, you dirty pervert. I forbid you to come near my daughter. I was told to be wary of you, but I would never have thought Juliette gullible enough to fall into your grubby paws."

Just then, the little girl appears at the end of the hallway, one arm in a sling, the other gesturing. Ferdinand can't make out if she's saying "what are you doing here?" or "I'll come by later" or even "sorry about my father . . ." But the door slams in Ferdinand's face, so he doesn't hear Antoine pick up the phone to call the police station.

Chapter Twenty-Three

Like a Ton of Bricks

There are days when nothing happens normally. Ferdinand will never forget that particular Friday.

Arm in a sling, and in spite of the formal ban on seeing that "sexual maniac" again, Juliette shows up at Ferdinand's door at 8:00 a.m., before going to school. On the doorstep, the little girl explains she had a fight with a boy in her class, Matteo Balard.

This "little nobody," as she calls him, dared to tell her that a woman's role is to be at home, waiting for her husband and catering to her children's every whim. According to him, only bad mothers work, the ones who don't love their children, and they usually end up running away from home. His father, Commissioner Balard, told him so, and the commissioner is always right. So a woman reporter, like Juliette's mother, boggles Matteo's mind. She must have problems at home to prefer going off to the other side of the world, to those war-torn countries. Not to mention her children, who must hate her. And the lovers she must have in every foreign city. A real slut, probably!

So Juliette had shoved Matteo and demanded he take back what he'd just said. The kid then spat in her face, grabbed her by the arm, and twisted it with all his might, until Juliette found herself on the ground, hunched in pain.

When Juliette finishes her story, the old man already knows he won't be able to let this stand.

Chapter Twenty-Four
Blowing a Gasket

Juliette has been at school for twenty minutes when Ferdinand hears the usual Friday morning grumbling of Mrs. Suarez, who is trying to carry the new vacuum cleaner—bagless but twice as heavy—to the top floor. Friday is sacred: dust must be eradicated before the weekend family visits. Mrs. Suarez loves to show off the perfectly maintained complex. Ferdinand, wanting to score some points before the next inspection, decides to lend a hand.

"Hello, Mrs. Suarez, you're looking lovely today. Is your skirt made of real crocodile?"

"Stand back. Can't you see you're in the way? This vacuum is heavy and I still have one more floor to go. Also, I can smell your cigar in the carpet fibers again. Are you doing it on purpose or what?"

"Let me help you, Mrs. Suarez. I can take a load off you and carry it to the top floor. It's no trouble. Give it here, you're going to break your back."

"Let go of that! Stop pulling . . . You're hurting me. I don't want your help, or your hypocrisy. I can't take any more of you! What would really take a load off me is seeing you leave. Fortunately, we'll soon be rid of you. For good!"

"With all due respect, Mrs. Suarez, don't get your hopes up. My daughter is a very wise woman. She asked me to make an effort, I have done so, and will continue to do so. Then she'll leave me alone about that retirement home. She keeps her word. She's a diplomat!"

"Poor old man, you understand nothing. You think you have control over your fate, but it escaped you months ago, while you still desperately cling to your pathetic little life. But it's over. This is the end for you!"

"You think you can scare me with so much hot air. Marion is a smart girl. She gets that from her father, you know!"

"Smart, maybe, but gullible, and easily manipulated. I can assure you! The poor little thing, so far away, and so worried. It's a good thing she has *me* to tell her the truth."

"What truth?"

"That you're making absolutely *no* effort! Your dental hygiene is deplorable—your toothbrush is at least ten years old. Your apartment is a dump and smells musty. Your food is worse than in the third world. I saw all the expired cans of preserves you ate and threw in the trash. With regard to friendliness, try again. You made Christine leave and have already insulted the new neighbor. As for your desire to live, pardon me, but setting fire to the trash area is too much! If you want to die, so be it, but leave the rest of us in peace!"

"Well, Mrs. Suarez, it's not at all what you think. The fire was to create a diversion because I wasn't ready to receive you that day. It wasn't to burn everything down, otherwise I would have turned on the gas!"

"You are a very sick man, Mr. Brun! Even worse than I thought. You don't even recognize the absurdity and danger of your actions. You need to get treatment. And what's more, I don't like you. You frighten me. You've already threatened me by telling me you'd cut me into pieces and toss them down the garbage chute. I could turn you in to the police, you know!"

"Just when I was starting to appreciate you and tell you things about my Pierre Bellemare books."

"Well, you have a funny way of showing people you appreciate them! Your place is not in this building—*my* building—but with the other old nutcases in the retirement home. And I'm going to see to it personally."

"Marion will never let that happen."

"You are so naïve, poor man! How do you think she found a place in a retirement home so quickly? I was the one who found the establishment—they owed me."

"Marion will never trust you when I tell her that."

"Marion *already* trusts me, and has for years. How do you like that, eh? She trusts me so much that she accepted my offer to do weekly reports on your movements. For free, too. Well, I didn't refuse the flat-screen TV she sent me for Christmas. The image quality is much better. Those Chinese are good at electronics!"

"This is too much. Too much! You won't get away with this, mark my words."

"It's too late, Mr. Brun. They're coming Monday. I've already called them. And it'll be just a formality with Marion. None of this would have happened if you'd known how to train your dog. My poor canaries . . . May they rest in peace."

"Leave Daisy alone. She never touched any of your damned birds."

"Well, she certainly touched that car. It didn't take long for her to pounce on the piece of steak I threw her. What a glutton! Beef back was her favorite cut, was it not?"

"What did you say? No, you didn't do that . . . Not to my Daisy! It was an accident, tell me it was an accident . . ."

Mrs. Suarez cackles like a hyena, another notorious scavenger.

"You deserve to die like your canaries . . . You old bitch!"

"Name-calling, that hardly surprises me about you, Mr. Brun. Shall I trot out 'old fossil' or 'born loser'? By the way, can we rent out your apartment during your prolonged absence? I have a good friend who would love to live in my complex. Now, if you'll excuse me, I have to do the stairwell."

Eyes bulging, hands ready to strangle, Ferdinand freezes, as if in a trance. When he comes to, he's alone, at home, wondering if the exchange really happened.

Chapter Twenty-Five

Over the Edge

If there's one thing Ferdinand can't stand, it's spinelessness. Attacking the weak is worst of all. First, Juliette, and on a whole other level, Daisy. The scum have no limits. He paces around his apartment, from one room to another, like a lion readying himself to encounter a new rival.

Ferdinand seeks revenge on Mrs. Suarez, but he hasn't devised the perfect plan yet. He dismisses his first ideas—pour rat poison through a funnel to stuff the silly old goose full, or grind her up in the garbage truck. But he risks getting caught and living out his days in prison, which is not the end he envisions for himself.

He has to get rid of her. He can no longer cross paths with her and listen to her honeyed, hypocritical voice without feeling like killing her, tearing out both her eyes, cutting out her lying viper's tongue. On further reflection, he may not have to attack her directly. Her husband? No, she doesn't give a rat's ass about him. But Rocco . . . In his younger days, Ferdinand learned how to butcher rabbits. It shouldn't be all that different for a Chihuahua. And it would please Mrs. Suarez so much to have a little souvenir, since she can't go out without her fur coat.

Given all these macabre ideas, Ferdinand knows there can't be a shared future in this complex. One of them has to go.

The old man is afraid to even leave his apartment. He's not sure what he's capable of should he come face-to-face with the concierge. The minimum would be spitting in her face before pushing her down the stairs. With a bit of luck, she'd snap her neck, and it could be passed off as an accident. Unless someone found his DNA on her face . . .

What if *he* turned *her* in to the police? Unfortunately, he has no proof, now that his dog has been reduced to ashes. And the silly old goose would deny everything or somehow turn the situation to her advantage and get him sent to jail.

Realizing he won't find any solutions within these walls, Ferdinand leaves, resigned to letting his impulses do the talking if he comes across the murderess. The concierge has finished with the vacuum and isn't in her loge. *She's hiding*, thinks Ferdinand. *Or else she's off stocking up at the butcher for her next massacre.* Ferdinand waits for her next to the trash bins.

Across from the complex is Juliette's elementary school. The poor child, with her arm in a sling . . . It must be difficult to do her writing assignments and multiplication tables.

12:15 p.m. The school bell rings. Ferdinand doesn't have time to register the meaning before a tide of book bags, each heavier than the last, tumbles out. It runs, it jostles; the gangs of boys don't pay any attention, shouldering past daydreaming girls who aren't moving fast enough. Ferdinand is dumbstruck by the sight of these larval human beings behaving like bullies. Especially those three guys, a short redhead and two big ones, two heads taller than he is. After insulting a group of older teenagers, they attack a lone girl in a skirt, the kind that flares when you twirl. The good-for-nothings try to lift it up. She begs, crying, "Stop it, Matteo, stop it! Tell your friends to let me go!"

Is there no one to defend this poor girl? Where are the teachers, the monitors? Ferdinand has never witnessed such a cruel spectacle between children. So he does what anyone else would do in his place: he looks elsewhere, pretending to be busy with something. Still no Mrs. Suarez on the horizon. Suddenly, shrill cries attract his attention. The three rascals are now forming a circle around their prey, who no longer knows where to turn. One of them grabs hold of the handle on her book bag and sends her flying two yards away. She skins her knee, bleeds, and starts sobbing. That's enough for today!

Ferdinand crosses the street in giant strides, seizes the lead brat by the collar, lifts him eight inches off the ground, crosses back to the complex, and stuffs his head in the nearest trash bin. The compost one.

"That's where you belong, you brat! I advise you never to pick on a girl again, or you'll have to deal with me. Ferdinand. And be careful, because I live here, across the street from your school, and I'll be watching you!"

The octogenarian looks up. The little girl has disappeared, while the two large boys lurk in a corner. Ferdinand has nothing left to do here. The morning's tension has fallen like a soufflé. He goes back to his apartment, where Juliette waits for him on the doormat. With this new twist in the Daisy affair, he forgot about their lunch, and with her father's prohibition, he thought she wouldn't come over anymore.

Juliette seems exhausted by her morning at school. She collapses onto the table, head resting heavily on her good elbow.

"Everything OK?" Ferdinand inquires.

Juliette replies with a weary groan. "No, it's that jerk Matteo again. He tore up the math lesson I'd just rewritten, which took me two hours with my left hand! I don't know what's keeping me from stabbing him in the hand with my compass so he gets the message."

Ferdinand sits down beside her and tells her, "Never answer violence with violence. You're smart, you'll always find something cleverer to bother him about. Above all, you must not get caught. We can think about it together if you want. For example, what's the thing he cares about most?"

Juliette scratches her head. "His grandmother, I think."

***

Mrs. Suarez is returning from her shopping when she discovers a pair of legs in her trash bins.

"What are you doing there, you scamp? Oh, heavens! Matteo, my darling! What happened to you? Tell Grandma . . ." She extracts the boy, muddy from the bin, and turns to a schoolgirl heading toward them. "And you, little girl, don't you know how to read? Your newspaper doesn't go in the compost bin. What are your glasses for? Paper goes in the yellow bin! No education these days, I'm telling you! Come along, Matteo, come here, my chick. We're going to clean you up."

It doesn't take Mrs. Suarez long to identify the lout who attacked her favorite grandson. "I'm calling your father, Matteo. He must be informed. You can't just attack a defenseless child with impunity! Not *my* grandson!"

Chapter Twenty-Six

The Last Straw

"All right, two across, six letters, *Greek tunic* . . . What's there already? I have *H, T, N* . . ." Beatrice pushes the plaid blanket away from her lap and stretches out her legs. Her fitness class at the gym the day before left her stiff. She turns to the pedestal table to the right of her armchair and grabs the thesaurus, her best friend for the *Figaro* crossword puzzles. "No, come on . . . Chiton! Of course, I should have thought of that! Where was my head? OK, now what's left?" While pondering, Beatrice taps her pencil, following the rapid tempo of *The Barber of Seville*.

The telephone rings, though she's not expecting any calls. It's 12:45 p.m. Who can it be? "Hello. Yes, this is she. No, you're not disturbing me. Shutters? It's nice of you to offer, but you see, I just had mine redone. Yes, throughout the apartment. Maybe even with your company, I don't recall anymore . . . Which company did you say you worked for? Yes, maybe it was them. Do you want me to check? Very well, as you wish. And a very nice day to you, too, sir."

Beatrice then remembers she was supposed to call Nespresso customer service back. She has visitors coming this weekend, and her coffeemaker is acting up. She retrieves her notepad and dials the number.

"Nespresso After-Sales Service, hello. How may I help you?"

"Hello, sir. My Nespresso machine is blinking and I can't make coffee anymore. It's quite annoying!"

"The three buttons on the machine are blinking? At the same time?"

"Yes."

"Well, ma'am, your problem is very common and quite simple to resolve. May I ask you to go stand next to your machine? Once you're there, press all three buttons at once, holding them down until you hear a very distinct 'click.' Go on, I'll wait."

Beatrice, doubtful, does so. She presses very hard for about twenty seconds, and there . . . Click!

"OK, ma'am, did you hear the noise?"

"I did."

"Very good. Now you can drain it and make coffee normally. Do you know how to drain the machine?"

"I do, yes."

"I'll wait while you check."

Beatrice performs the action, and brownish water flows out. It's a good sign. Once the capsule is engaged, steaming coffee flows like magic from the device. Perfect.

"Sir? Everything is working like before. You're effective over there at Nespresso. It's a surprising repair technique, pushing three buttons at once, but as long as it works and it's simple, it's fine with me. Thank you for your patience, sir. Have a lovely day."

Beatrice pours a cup of lukewarm coffee. She doesn't feel like drinking it before lunch, but it mustn't be wasted. She gulps down the espresso, then realizes she could have heated it in the microwave after her meal. Oh, well.

With coffee-stained teeth and a pasty tongue, Beatrice gets back to her crossword. She spends a quarter of an hour looking for a synonym for her second-to-last word, when the telephone rings again.

"Hello? Yes, this is she. A bathtub? No, thank you. Yes, I know they can be dangerous past a certain age. That's why I have side handles installed along mine. Yes, I have all I need. No, don't bother offering me another discount. Good-bye, ma'am. Have a nice day."

Beatrice is tired of these daily calls coming in one after the other. But at the same time, it's unthinkable for her not to answer. What if it were an emergency?

Beatrice decides to fix herself a good, simple meal consisting of a raw zucchini salad with balsamic vinaigrette, lemon cod with basmati rice, and for dessert, her guilty pleasure: a chocolate éclair!

She's preparing the fish, when the telephone rings again. She hesitates, then heaves a big sigh and picks up the receiver.

"Yes? No. My Internet connection works very well, ma'am. Yes, I'm very satisfied with it. No, there's no reason to change it today. No, I'm not interested in your offer. I'm sorry. I have to go, ma'am. Good day to you, too."

What irritates her the most is that now her fish is cold, and if she reheats it, it will be overdone, like it always is at restaurants. She returns to the kitchen and heats up a lemon sauce, then coats the fish with it. It's saved! The cod is delicious. *I won't have any need for sea bream anymore. I'll praise the fishmonger for his advice.*

The old lady glances at the clock. 1:45 p.m. *Quick, it's about to start.* She takes her dessert and goes into the living room. TNT is so convenient; she can watch old episodes of *Agatha Christie, Murder, She Wrote*, or *Columbo*. With relish, Beatrice devours her dessert without missing a second of the detective story.

After reading thirty pages of the book selected by Mrs. Granger for their book club, which, as always, is turning out to be torture, Beatrice takes care of her little chores. Thus begins the auditing of her accounts, documenting every expenditure and every bill received. Next, Beatrice consults her bank account online to verify the debits have been subtracted. For more than seventy years, Beatrice has balanced her checkbook daily, and in seventy years, only twice has she found errors—errors that were, both times, in her favor!

By reading her account books, one could follow her life like a personal diary. Her spending on food at the market or the wine expo, her purchases of flowers for her weekly visits to retirement homes or burials, her checks written for birthday gifts for her grandchildren, her outings to the theater, to the movies, to the museum. And especially her travels all over the world. There is no continent Beatrice hasn't seen, no major church in a capital city she hasn't admired, seemingly no train station or airport in which she hasn't had a layover. She is fully informed on Middle Eastern geopolitics, Asian funeral traditions, African tribal history, South American culinary specialties, and even sub-Arctic fauna. Beatrice always has extraordinary stories to tell about her journeys. Bus trips through war-torn countries; river crossings that resulted in emergency evacuations to lifeboats; perilous flights on the first recreational aircraft—attempting to land on runways that five minutes earlier had been fruit and vegetable markets. Beatrice enjoyed sushi, enchiladas, and pizza well before anyone else did. She's even met the pope twice—well, two different pontiffs.

Yes, Beatrice has been lucky. She's made wonderful memories, though it's true she's started to forget them little by little, to mix them up. So she's taken to labeling each object with a number that refers to a detailed explanation in a little notebook: date, place, travel companions, context, and anecdote. Every day, she travels through time to a distant country, searching the depths of her memory for the extraordinary stories she can pass on. When she hosts her grandchildren, it's with pleasure that she relates one of the journeys, often with wide eyes and laughter.

Beatrice says that when she's finished her labeling, she'll start on the family's Super 8 movies. Certain films from the period between the wars have even been used in documentaries.

But Beatrice's life hasn't always been rosy. She's the last surviving sibling among seven, and the surviving member of the happy couple she once formed with Georges, taken much too soon, more than fifty years ago. Beatrice raised her children by herself, learned how to rustle up the money she needed, how to cope with the growing solitude as her nearest and dearest disappeared. To counter the devastating effects of time, Beatrice strives to infuse her days with new blood, and, if possible, young blood. She tries to make herself as useful as possible—to the parish, to her neighbors, to her family. She wants to help those around her before she goes.

Careful to make her letters round and clear, Beatrice spends hours bent over her notebook choosing the right words, remembering the story exactly. On this particular day, she's recording some memories of the immense, dark painting over the mantel, which depicts the portrait of a marshal of the Empire, a family ancestor. It's a strange story of the forefather being condemned and pardoned, and the painting being stolen, then lost, and finally bought back.

In the growing shadows, she suddenly realizes it's already 6:10 p.m. Good God! The show! She drops everything and runs to her armchair. Julien appears on the screen. She grumbles, realizing she's missed the beginning of *Questions for a Champion*. She turns up the volume and leans forward to better hear the questions. She generally gets the answers before the contestants, whom she then berates with insulting names.

Beatrice has gotten four answers in a row when she turns, hackles up, eyes fixed on the phone, which is ringing. During *Questions for a Champion*! In one leap, Beatrice jumps up, picks up the receiver, and slams it back down. Then she takes the telephone off the hook.

"Honestly! During *my* show. Now I've seen everything! People are really inconsiderate. Well, that's nice, I missed the last qualifier!"

Across the landing, behind Ferdinand's door, the same frenzy prevails. On the upper floors, as well. All of a sudden, the volume on all the televisions in the building is turned up by at least ten clicks. It's time for "Four in a Row." You could shout, scream, wail . . . no one would hear anything. Say, isn't that Mrs. Suarez hollering from the trash area, calling for help with all her strength?

The contestant has just gotten four points in a row! Everyone shouts with joy—Julien Lepers, the contestant, Ferdinand, and all the grandmothers at their posts.

Chapter Twenty-Seven

Each More Than the Last

There are days when everything smiles at you, when the planets align.

While Mrs. Suarez is very ill and very, very far away (that is, at the hospital following a heart attack), Ferdinand discovers among his mail an exquisite invitation to lunch from Mrs. Claudel. She requests that he join her "in all simplicity" to share lunch the next day, a Saturday, to recover together from the emotional past several weeks.

It's been decades since Ferdinand was invited to lunch. The octogenarian is flattered because he knows how important weekend lunches are to his neighbor. He wonders if he'll be good company. What does she talk about with her grandchildren? Literature, movies, travel?

Ferdinand panics. He's already not the talkative type. Mrs. Claudel is the sort to talk enough for two, but she seems to have a high opinion of him, and would expect him to say something, though he has nothing to offer. He's even lied to her, notably when he asked for help regarding the housekeeper. He's afraid she'll discover he's not interested in much, or at least anything he'd like to share on a first date.

His life stopped when his wife left him. Louise would say it had stopped years earlier, when Marion left, that moment when couples realize they have nothing in common without their child. Plus Ferdinand is about as old as the hills, and Beatrice talks about things on the Internet that he doesn't understand. In any case, what's the point of trying? At his age, learning is meaningless. Unless he really does have ten years left to live . . .

Chapter Twenty-Eight

A Real Lady-Killer

The Sunday following lunch with Mrs. Claudel isn't a day like any other: everything must be perfect. Ferdinand wants to show himself in the best light. He opens his closet and chooses a brown checked shirt, ironed and put away a long, long time ago. He unfolds it. A musty smell wafts up. Isn't it a bit too large now? A little cologne will take care of the first problem. As for the second, the jacket will hide the turned-up sleeves. The pair of clean, pleat-front pants is all set. The jacket will be his everyday one, because Ferdinand doesn't have any others. A bow tie will bring the whole look together. But where is that damned tie? He hasn't used it since . . . his wedding! Fifty-eight years ago? *Oh my, not the time to think about that.*

Underneath a mountain of clothes—each piece more faded and holey than the last—is a brown velvet bow tie, which has been resting in peace for more than half a century. Doubt suddenly strikes him. Will Ferdinand remember how to tie the knot? He stands in front of the mirror, hung by its chain on the window's *espagnolette* lock. His eyes have darker circles beneath them than usual; a pink scar sweeps across his right jawline, a souvenir from his bus accident. He looks a fright, but it could be worse. His complexion isn't as pale as he's used to. He did well to snag a little of Beatrice's tanner on the sly.

He ties the velvet bow around his shirt collar and contemplates the result: the monochromatic browns suit him to a T. All that's missing is a little blue to bring out his eyes. His cloth handkerchief, which is usually lodged in the pocket of his gray sweatpants, takes up residence in the front pocket of his jacket. And voilà! Ferdinand is ready. And stressed out. What if nothing goes as planned? *Come on, come on, get a grip, Ferdinand! Now's not the time to lose your nerve.*

Summoning his courage, and holding the roses by their stems, the thorns determined to leave him with an indelible memory of this day, Ferdinand walks the five yards that separate his door from the one he's so often spied upon. He rings the doorbell. Not a sound from inside. He rings a second time. Nothing. On the fourth ring, the door opens at last, revealing a terribly drowsy Beatrice in a pale pink wool bathrobe. Her eyes, without glasses, open wide upon seeing Ferdinand.

***

Beatrice has never seen Ferdinand like this, wearing something other than his perpetual shapeless brown pants. She's never seen a proper shirt on Ferdinand, either, let alone what appears to be a bow tie—not very conventional these days, but it's the idea that counts.

However, what touches the old lady is the awkwardness and fragility radiating from him. He has an almost stupid expression: smile plastered to his lips, eyes benevolent and soft. But what's more unexpected is his hair. It's back to being brown overnight. Out with the Bill Clinton–style white! In with the Silvio Berlusconi brown!

"What's going on, Ferdinand? Why are you ringing my bell at seven thirty in the morning? Has there been a problem since our lunch yesterday? Did the sushi give you indigestion? Still annoyed you didn't manage to eat with chopsticks? I'm teasing you. You look . . . strange," continues Beatrice, noticing the orange spots on his face, as if he had spent time under a defective UV lamp.

"No, on the contrary, everything's fine. It's been a long time since I've felt so good! Here. These are flowers. I didn't quite know what to get. I know you buy a lot of chrysanthemums, but the florist suggested roses."

"You shouldn't have. You're crazy! Is there a special reason, Ferdinand? Come sit in the living room."

"I don't really know how to tell you what I've come here to say, but, uh . . ."

"Then say nothing. I get it."

"Really?"

Seated on the sofa, Ferdinand moves his hand toward Beatrice's. Their wrinkled fingers brush against each other. Ferdinand looks at Beatrice tenderly, and she smiles at him. The scene is comical: an old lady in a bathrobe hosting a gentleman of a certain age dressed to the nines, timidly touching the tips of their fingers together.

Beatrice draws her hand back suddenly.

"No, Ferdinand. No! You've shown me that in life it's sometimes preferable to say no. Today I owe you that honesty. This is not a good idea, and deep down, I'm sure you know it, too. I've lost too many friends, and then heaven sends me a fantastic person. I refuse to lose you, too. We've lived long enough, the both of us, to know that love stories end badly."

"But we have so much in common . . ."

"And we'll continue to. I don't want that to change. Love, that's not for me anymore. And let's be reasonable—I'm much too old for you. You've told me yourself that your type are the pretty young things fifty years old!"

"I thought so, too, but—"

"Ferdinand, no. I'm touched, really I am, and also a bit embarrassed. But I love only one man now: God. I'm still delighted to see that your heart has learned to love again. When you're ready, I could introduce you to lots of my lady friends from the retirement home, but only one of them is your type—she looks like Claire Chazal . . ."

"Oh, no, not those crazy old ladies. They're too old. They're all at least eighty! It's you, Beatrice, who pleases me, and if you tell me no, that's it for us. I'll be more alone than ever."

Beatrice gets up and heads for the door.

"Don't speak such nonsense, my dear man. I'm sorry but I have to get ready now. My grandchildren are coming over for lunch and I need to be at the market when it opens to find some cod. We'll see each other on Tuesday for our card game. I'm counting on you. Don't let our friends come over for a three-person bridge party! And promise me one thing: don't put on your Ferdinand act. Stop crossing things off as soon as they don't turn out the way you want. You have to learn to swallow your pride sometimes. To know how to lose. All right, see you Tuesday. Our new player will be there. Good-bye, Ferdinand!"

Ferdinand finds himself on the threshold of Beatrice's door, roses in hand and heart on his sleeve. That damned bridge party. He won't go. It's over with Beatrice!

Ferdinand goes back home, humiliated. He doesn't understand how he misinterpreted her signals. They were so clear. She gave him come-hither eyes! He was sure of it. Or is she one of those women who constantly changes her mind?

What bothers him the most is that he's going to have to move. He has his pride, and he can no longer cross paths with her every day on the landing. There are a lot of people to avoid! Mrs. Suarez, Beatrice . . . But the real question is, where will he go? From the other side of the door, you'd think you were listening to a telephone conversation. "I don't have anywhere else to go. It would be more practical if Beatrice was the one to go, right? She has a beach house. And if I leave, Juliette will be sad. I'm like the grandfather she never had. And fine, I'd miss her, too. I really like that kid. She has a certain je ne sais quoi that reminds me of myself at her age. I'd pass on her family, but that little girl . . . She'll fare well in life. I just hope she'll be happier and luckier in love than I was.

"But what did I do to the Good Lord for life to dog me so? What did I do to deserve this? Could anything worse happen to me?"

Chapter Twenty-Nine

The Goose Is Cooked

On Monday, once lunch with Juliette is over, Ferdinand settles into his armchair and pulls the blanket up over his legs. A lukewarm cup of coffee in hand, he listens to the radio. Every day, at 2:00 p.m., his favorite program, *True Crime*, starts. He wouldn't miss an episode for anything in the world. However, he has trouble following the detective stories to the end, digestion often getting the better of him. He loves the sensation of weightlessness, of dizziness, that envelops him at naptime. He also loves the warmth of waking up, his slow state of half-consciousness. His postlunch naps constitute his best sleep, as his nights are often short.

Today, the program reexamines "The Case of the Red Sweater," a classic. The enigmatic piece of clothing has just been discovered as Ferdinand, drowsy, snuggles farther into the soft cushions. The investigation moves forward, the shocking testimony piles up, his eyelids grow heavy. A suspect is identified, the police conduct a search, yelling, "Police, open up! I know you're in there!" Ferdinand descends into a warm torpor. The police threaten to break down the door; the suspect doesn't open up despite blows that make the walls shake. Ferdinand tries to resist, he knows he's going to miss the end of the story and Ranucci's death sentence—one of the last Frenchmen to be guillotined. Too bad, he remembers the case perfectly, except that the suspect was also named Ferdinand . . .

The case stalls. The police still can't get into the suspect's home. "Open up, Ferdinand, open up!" The amount of time spent in front of that door starts to bore him. The policeman's summons is unconvincing. "Police! Open up. Ferdinand, open up. It's Eric. I know you're in there. It's time for your radio program."

Christian! Ranucci's name was Christian. In the very depths of his unconsciousness, that information seems important, but Ferdinand no longer knows why. All of a sudden, his cup—which had remained in his hand—tips over. Ferdinand then realizes that a raving lunatic is in the midst of banging away at the door. *His* door. The old man stands still and straight as an arrow, a foot and a half from the intruder trying to gain entrance to his home.

"Police! Open up, Ferdinand. It's Eric. I know you're in there. I heard you walking around."

Dumbfounded, the old man closes his eyes to pull himself together, then protests, "How do you like that for manners? The police just start breaking down your door 'cause you don't open it fast enough. I was having a little snooze—that's still legal in

France, isn't it? The police are so damn lovely! What are you doing at my place, Super Cop? I'm an honest citizen. You can leave now, Eric. I'm not letting you in. No way I'm going to your cursed home for old fools. I made the effort Marion asked me to, no matter what report the old goose might've given to get rid of me. You can't detain someone by force!"

In a menacing voice, Eric retorts, "Well, that's what we're going to find out. I have a warrant for your arrest. If you don't let me in, I'll enter by force."

Ferdinand isn't the least bit impressed.

"Is that so? They're sending the police now, and with an arrest warrant to boot. All that just to fill the retirement homes! Nice profession. The police have fallen far." Ferdinand opens the door. "You can make your inspection. Everything's spic-and-span, like Marion wanted. I don't know what Mrs. Suarez made up this time. I scoured every room from top to bottom. Fine, I just spilled some coffee, but the fridge is full, I took a bath yesterday, I helped Mrs. Claudel carry up her groceries. And I'm doing very well, better than I have in a long time."

"I'm happy for you, but there's been a misunderstanding. I've come to take you down to the station, not to look over the premises."

"To the station?"

"You've been accused of the murder of Mrs. Suarez. Two witnesses have come forward and they're positive you explicitly and publicly threatened Mrs. Suarez with death less than twelve hours before she died."

Eric pulls Ferdinand out of the apartment and takes out the handcuffs.

"Please come quietly." Noting the attention of bystanders gathering on the stairs, he calls out, "Everybody return to your homes. Let the police do their work, thank you."

Hands cuffed behind his back and urged to move forward, Ferdinand tries to understand. "Is this a bad joke? Am I on hidden camera? What murder? What witnesses? Mrs. Suarez isn't dead—she had a heart attack and is under observation at the hospital!"

"That would suit you, but no. Mrs. Suarez didn't survive. Now we have a death, which to us seems intentional, and the evidence is working against you. The medical examiner will issue his report soon, which we expect will confirm our suspicions. And *you'll* spend the rest of your days rotting in prison. The retirement home wasn't so bad as all that, eh?" finishes Eric, with a vindictive little smile.

Chapter Thirty

In a Sticky Situation

There's a first time for everything in life, but spending more than twelve hours in a cold, damp, claustrophobic cell isn't on the list of things Ferdinand wishes to do before he dies. At first he shares his custody with a drunk homeless man, who has the good fortune to be released. As for his own fate, no one deigns to keep him informed. Nevertheless, the old man is confident this is just a gross misunderstanding and, very shortly, the commissioner, or even the chief of police himself, will come running and flatly apologize for this regrettable mistake. But for the time being, no one has come to rescue him. For more than twelve hours now, he's been waiting, straightening up at every round of hurried steps—hope gradually eroding, knowing nothing of what plots are hatching on the outside.

And indeed Eric, the Super Cop, has done his work: neither the commissioner nor the chief of police would fly to the aid of a murderous old man. Eric's best collar in the past five years, according to his superior. They are still waiting for confirmation of the murder, which will come from the examination of the body. The suspect's confession should follow without a hitch. For the moment, they are applying the technique of neglect.

Ferdinand has the right to make a single phone call. He should have remembered that Marion isn't the best at picking up, but her number is the only one he knows by heart. Marion, true to form, hadn't answered. Be that as it may, she could always listen to the message, "Uh, Marion . . . it's me. Pick up, please. It's an emergency. I'm at the police station because of the concierge. You've got to call a lawyer for me as soon as possible."

The policeman who escorted Ferdinand to his cell snickers. "I told you to call a lawyer. It's nighttime in Asia. Nothing's going to happen for . . . eight hours at least. You're in trouble, old man. Deep trouble. What's more, they don't let maniacs like you get out easily. You're gonna get forty-eight hours in police custody, man. Going after a poor defenseless lady for some business about canaries? No need to be so final. Then to shout it from the rooftops beforehand? I hope your daughter cares about you and listens to her messages." The policeman steals all hope from him. Why had he chosen Marion? Why couldn't he have called someone else? He has no friends. Nobody who cares enough about him. And most importantly, nobody who's aware of what he's been subjected to for more than thirteen hours now . . .

Ferdinand is thirsty, hungry, and sleepy, though he normally tosses and turns before falling into the arms of Morpheus. He's lost track of the sequence of events and is going crazy. They're still telling him nothing. He calls out, he shouts. His screams must be reaching somebody! Unless they've all gone home. Ferdinand starts to feel faint. "A glass of water, I need a glass of water!" He slaps the bars. In the distance, someone replies that old people are never thirsty. Everybody knows that, since they didn't even get thirsty enough to drink the water they needed during the last heat wave.

Ferdinand continues to shout. He has no more saliva. He's exhausting himself, and no one's coming. Now he feels cold. He lets himself slide to the floor, back against the bars, curls up, and gradually sinks into a restless sleep.

He's on an idyllic beach, alone. The sun warms him. Ferdinand is dazzled; he can no longer distinguish the glittering of the ocean, as he's been staring at it for hours. The sky is postcard blue. Seagulls take to the air, followed by cormorants. A few yards in front of him, a fat lizard basks in the sun. *The good life*, thinks Ferdinand, shading his eyes with his hand to look at the horizon. Startled, the lizard runs away. In the distance, goats bleat and strike against the fences of their pen. A boat approaches the coast as the sun hides behind a cloud. Ferdinand looks up. The cloud is black, gigantic. The old man sees more clearly now. It's not a boat coming nearer. It's much too fast. And much too big.

Suddenly, the ocean retreats as fast as a galloping horse. The lagoon dries within seconds. Then a monumental wave more than fifty feet high rises up. Ferdinand's mouth goes dry. His heart races. He barely knows how to swim, but he doesn't have any more time to think. He takes a breath, the deepest he can, just as the full force of the wave crashes into him.

Ferdinand is pulled into the depths, whirling and thrown in every direction. His arm collides with a tree trunk. Air. Quickly, air! He opens his mouth and manages to get a few gulps at the surface, in between rolls, when suddenly the pain in his arm becomes sharper, like a bite . . .

He discovers a man bending over him, pulling on his arm. He's wearing a uniform. It's a policeman holding a cup. Ferdinand, semiconscious, grabs it and drinks greedily, letting half of it flow down his chin. He chokes and coughs, but his thirst is finally quenched. His heart is racing two thousand miles an hour. Ferdinand isn't sure where he is. Where did the wave go?

The policeman stretches out a hand to Ferdinand to help him up. "Pull yourself together, old man, it's time. Your little fainting fit is nothing compared to what you've got coming. The commissioner is waiting for you. I don't know what you did to him, but it seems he has it out for you!"

Chapter Thirty-One

For Heaven's Sake

When Ferdinand enters the office of the commissioner—who is leaning back in his pleather armchair, hands behind his head and eyes hollow—Ferdinand gets the impression he is disturbing him. Commissioner Balard, in his forties, points to one of the wooden chairs in front of his desk. Ferdinand sits down. The policeman who escorted him in remains standing in a corner of the room. The old man is outnumbered. A rather unpleasant feeling. The commissioner stands abruptly, turns to the window, obstructed by dust-gray blinds, then turns and leans toward him, staring him right in the eyes.

"Mr. Brun, you are accused of the premeditated homicide of Mrs. Suarez. Are you aware of the facts alleged against you?"

"I have the right to a lawyer, Mr. Commissioner. I'll tell you everything you want to know when he's here."

"And did you call this lawyer? No! So you must not need one. So let's start again. You don't seem to understand the gravity of the situation. Mrs. Suarez was found Saturday morning, around nine fifteen, in the trash area, unconscious. At the hospital she only lasted two days. That still means nothing to you? Allow me to refresh your memory. You had a dispute with Mrs. Suarez on Friday morning. I have two witnesses who swear to it. Voices were raised, you grabbed her and threatened to kill her. I quote: 'You'll pay for what you've done.' Not very nice. And as if by chance, she has a fatal accident the next day. I'll tell you what I really think: it wasn't an accident and you know it, Mr. Brun! You were there, you were waiting for her in the trash area, and you did irreparable damage."

"I'm entitled to a court-appointed lawyer, and he's not here. I can't answer your questions without him, sir."

"That's 'Commissioner Balard'! And that's enough of your acting! You watch too much TV. In a minute you're going to tell me about the Fifth Amendment. We're not in a TV soap opera. This is real life. There's been a murder and we're waiting for your explanation!"

Ferdinand is impassive, eyes staring into space, arms dangling. It's not that he's playing games, but he's had nothing to eat for more than a day, and he wouldn't react even if they spit on him. He doesn't have the energy to raise his voice, to explain himself. The only thing he can hang on to is his knowledge. His detective novels, his afternoons listening to the radio, his years of lunches with Super Cop. He knows he has rights, notably the rights to remain silent and to the presence of a lawyer.

But he also knows he's not going to last long against the commissioner. No court-appointed lawyer was called or will come save him like magic. If the commissioner wants a battle of wits, or worse, to play hardball, he's done for. Ferdinand knows the commissioner's type: he'll keep pushing, first with words, then physically. How many stories has he read about innocent suspects confessing after endless harsh interrogations? Only for the real culprits to be discovered decades later, when the poor men have languished in prison their whole lives—or worse. That's what he's got coming. He knows it. Might makes right.

Ferdinand comes back to his senses and finds the commissioner bright red, his forehead vein throbbing. He's mangling a poor sheet of paper, which, a few seconds earlier, had recounted the progression of the investigation. Ferdinand understands that that's it, things are serious. The interrogation will turn personal and become a settling of scores. He hears voices outside the office. Damn! Balard has called for reinforcements.

The office door opens. A figure Ferdinand knows all too well appears.

***

"Well, I never—what kind of manners are these? Nobody pushes me, Mrs. Claudel, Esquire, Mr. Brun's lawyer. I was kept at the reception desk for over an hour by a certain Eric. I've been prevented from attending the interrogation of my client, which has already begun. That's illegal, Mr. Commissioner. And I would have appreciated being let in without all the searches. I'm not hiding explosives in my cane, for God's sake!"

At the word *explosives*, worried looks pass between the commissioner and his men. Balard is taken aback: he hadn't foreseen this, just when he was about to get down to business. Within a few moments, the atmosphere changes. The old lady takes over the place, from her smelly perfume, to her handbag on his files, to her cane, which she taps at every turn to draw attention. The commissioner tries to regain control.

"Ma'am, under no circumstance would we keep you longer than necessary. It's normal procedure. With all due respect, how long has it been since you practiced?"

"Shouldn't you cede your place in the interrogation, Mr. Commissioner? There's a conflict of interest when the victim is the commissioner's mother-in-law," replies Beatrice Claudel without missing a beat.

The party's just getting started . . .

"Mrs. Claudel, your client is looking at fifteen years. That is, he'll never see the light of day again. We have two witnesses swearing he threatened the life of Mrs. Suarez; he has a motive—some sordid story about a dog and canaries. Plus, there is his suspicious behavior, with the comings and goings in the complex's trash area, and intimidation via books detailing murderers' physical abuse. Not to mention inappropriate behavior with young children!"

"Have you finished?" The commissioner nods, and Beatrice Claudel continues. "I see nothing but speculation, Mr. Commissioner. So, if you don't mind, let's concentrate on the death of Mrs. Suarez and proceed with the facts. Nothing but the facts, Mr. Commissioner. I have here the medical examiner's report, prepared just two hours ago. It confirms a natural death via heart attack. There is nothing astonishing about that for a woman who has been in the care of a cardiologist, Dr. Bernardin, for more than fifteen years. But you already knew that, Mr. Commissioner. Mrs. Suarez had been taking ASA, acetylsalicylic acid, and perindopril, a hypotensive, every day for eight years to reduce the risk of a cardiac event. I have here a copy of her prescriptions. Mrs. Suarez had several times charged me with picking up her medications, on days when she was too weak to leave her loge. As an oversight, I kept the prescription at the bottom of my bag. There are so many useless things knocking about in a woman's handbag, Mr. Commissioner. As you can see, she picked up her medications at the pharmacy on Rue Bonaparte every month. The pharmacist can confirm that.

"Furthermore, Mrs. Suarez's cardiac problems were taken very seriously by her doctor, given her family history. Her mother and aunt each had a myocardial infarction, at fifty-three and fifty-five years of age, respectively. They did not survive. Mrs. Suarez was fifty-seven. You will find here the death certificates and a note from Dr. Bernardin. I should point out that he is not infringing on any patient confidentiality, since these certificates were given to Mrs. Suarez so that she would be aware of potential risks."

Balard can't help but laugh richly and begins to put an end to the charade, when Beatrice, with a tap of her cane, takes over once more.

"Next, the time of death. The medical examiner places it between nine o'clock and nine thirty on Monday morning at the hospital, after her heart attack on Friday evening. Did you ask my client if he has an alibi? Do you have proof he was at the scene? Well, I'll tell you. Mr. Brun, present here, was at the post office sending a package to his grandson for his birthday. The employees are precise: he arrived at the Garibaldi office around 8:55. He then used the ATM at 9:28. I have a copy of the receipt. He took out seventy euros, then left on foot. The grocer is adamant that Mr. Brun was the first one that day to buy chanterelles.

"In short, Mr. Brun's busy life is not, it seems, the object of his arrest. Therefore, Mr. Commissioner, I ask you: since the medical examiner confirms the natural death as a result of a heart attack, and since my client has numerous alibis, what are we doing here? Why was my client kept in prison for over twenty hours? Why was he locked up under conditions that defy comprehension? Why?"

"Mr. Brun is wanted for premeditated homicide, following the testimony of two witnesses. For the moment, we prefer to keep their identities a secret."

"Ah, the witnesses! How reliable! No need to tell me the names of the two neighbor ladies in question. Mrs. Joly, a notorious alcoholic, who has replaced her morning tea with Floc de Gascogne liqueur for years. We all know she stays cooped up in her home, the third-floor stairs having already given her a memorable fall.

When Mr. Brun supposedly had words with Mrs. Suarez, Mrs. Joly was already drunk. Next, the second witness, Mrs. Berger, known by the police to be a kleptomaniac, has a grudge against my client, more precisely against the late Daisy, Mr. Brun's dog. Her Persian cat was scared stiff of that dog. She'd tried to give rat poison to Daisy, who had refused the piece of meat. I saw it with my own eyes. I don't ask you to believe me. I invite you to check your witness's alibi. You will discover that when she claims to have heard a dispute, she was being held in the back room of the Franprix supermarket on Rue Bourseau for stealing mascara. They kept her there until she agreed to pay, at closing, at 7:00 p.m. So I ask you, Mr. Commissioner, do you have irrefutable proof against my client?"

Balard glances around for support from his men, but they all duck their heads.

"I'll take your silence as a no. Therefore, nothing whatsoever is detaining my client. I hope not to see you again soon. Good day!"

With these words, Beatrice stands up and grasps Ferdinand's arm, supporting him on the way to the office door.

As they're exiting, the commissioner says, "Be sure to pay the one-hundred-and-thirty-five euro fine for unauthorized parking in a handicapped spot." Beatrice shoots daggers at him, and the commissioner hastens to add, "I'm joking, obviously." He immediately side-eyes his colleague, causing the man to rush off.

"I don't doubt it," retorts Beatrice. "Trampling my client's rights was sufficient. You couldn't have intended for a man over eighty, dehydrated and hypoglycemic, to walk over three hundred feet. Good day!" Beatrice turns to Ferdinand. "I'm not kidding, my friend. You're in bad shape. We're going to the hospital. You must see a doctor immediately. We'll have them verify the terrible treatment and then we'll see who's paying far more than one hundred and thirty-five euros!"

***

Beatrice helps the old man into her black Mini. A true exercise in contortion for the tall Ferdinand, already worn out. Without putting on her seat belt, Beatrice tears out of the parking lot and onto the road, not taking the slightest glance at traffic. Ferdinand immediately buckles his seat belt and clings to the door handle.

"Slow down, Mrs. Claudel. It's not an emergency."

"Mrs. Claudel? Since when do you no longer call me Beatrice? Poor dear! They really turned your brain. And you haven't seen your face! You're white as a sheet, even paler than you were before."

"I'd feel better if you slowed down. Maybe you should let me drive."

"In your condition? We'd be ripe for an accident! Oh, shoot, we just missed the exit. Look out your side and tell me if anyone's coming."

"You're going to back up on the freeway?"

"Is anyone there or not? No one? I'm going!"

Beatrice shifts into reverse for fifty yards to get to the access ramp leading to the hospital. She takes the corner, pedal to the metal.

"I mean it! Slow down or we're gonna die!"

"Isn't that what you wanted, after all? I'm kidding, my dear. No, seriously, we've had car accidents in my family. My husband was a Formula 3 driver and he died during a training run, may he rest in peace. And one of my nephews got himself run over by a bus in England. He looked the wrong way and died on the spot. So believe me, I am extremely careful. Stay buckled up, though, we just went through a stale yellow light."

In the distance, the glowing *H* of the hospital appears. Ferdinand breathes a sigh of relief. Only a few more yards. At fifty miles per hour, Beatrice charges into the parking lot and comes to a stop with a controlled skid, in the area reserved for emergencies.

Totally bananas, concludes Ferdinand.

"Look, we're safe and sound. Come on, let's hurry."

Getting out, Ferdinand staggers. He leans against the car for a moment and ascertains the extent of previous damage to the car: right side pushed in, rear bumper dented, and scratches just about everywhere. Yes, indeed, Beatrice is extremely cautious in a car.

Chapter Thirty-Two

Nutty as a Fruitcake

The room Ferdinand is consigned to is twice as small as the one he had during his previous stay at the hospital—and twice as inhabited. To his right, a little eighty-year-old dame with the look of an over-the-hill TV news anchor makes it known she's more than delighted to have company. Ferdinand, meanwhile, struggles with the stiff neck that's resulted from snubbing his neighbor's idle chatter and keeping his head turned toward the window. He's waiting for the medical team to remember his existence, when finally the tall white figure of Dr. Labrousse enters.

"Ah, Doctor! There you are. Can you get me out of here? I can't take it anymore. My skull hurts. My roommate does nothing but talk. And very loudly at that. Is she deaf or what? Do something, please."

"Mrs. Petit? Isn't she adorable? Always a funny story to tell."

"That's what you think. Try sharing a room with her and you tell me whether you appreciate hearing the same two stories on a loop. Then at night, how she coughs! Is whatever she's got contagious? What's she in for?"

"A fall in her kitchen. I assure you, she's getting out soon. RIGHT, MRS. PETIT? HAPPY TO BE LEAVING?" Then Dr. Labrousse turns back to Ferdinand. "I'm going to tell you a secret: she's got a crush on you. She told all the nurses and her grandchildren that you look like Clint Eastwood or Anthony Hopkins, only more mature."

"I'm not sure that's a compliment. A cross between a trigger-happy cop and a cannibal? Thanks so much! Can't you switch my room? Or better, allow me to leave? It's been more than two days. I feel like I'm going to catch a hospital-acquired infection."

"Calm down, Mr. Brun. First of all, how is your jaw doing?"

"Fine. But what am I doing here? I feel great, apart from this damned pain in my skull." He sends a dark look toward the neighboring bed. "I want to go home. They're keeping me without explanation."

"Rest assured, it's nothing serious, Mr. Brun. We just want to get you back on your feet and use the time to do some supplementary testing."

"No wonder the hole in the social services budget is so big. Who's paying for these tests no one needs? Not me, I hope."

"No, it's not you, Mr. Brun. I have to say, I'm rather surprised by the results of your analyses."

"You were surprised last time, too," Ferdinand retorts, impassive, recalling his days after the bus incident.

"Yes, but positively that time. What's surprising me today is the weakness in your heart. Have you done anything crazy lately? I'm trying to understand what could have changed in such a short time."

"I don't rightly know. I just took a ride here in a car the size of a yogurt cup at Formula 1 speeds, driven not by Michael Schumacher, but by a blind nonagenarian who's unaware of the dangers. Maybe it's that?"

"Hmm, I don't think so. In any case, we're going to have to take care of you. Take it easy. Get yourself pampered by your family, and avoid pointless physical exertion, emotional shocks, and ill-advised romps with Mrs. Petit. I'm joking! Come on, I'll give you something to quiet your migraine and if everything checks out tonight, you'll be gone tomorrow morning. Take heart, Mr. Brun!"

Chapter Thirty-Three

Going to Confession

The medication prescribed by Dr. Labrousse to relieve the headache turns out to be effective—so effective that Ferdinand no longer hears his neighbor's ramblings. He can't even tell whether she's still in the room or if he's been transported elsewhere.

Ferdinand feels good, like he's floating on a little cloud, cradled by an all-encompassing warmth. He begins to daydream, to wander. Life seems so sweet all of a sudden. It's one of those moments when you tell yourself to pause here, to leave the bookmark in your life at this precise instant. Even though he's at the hospital—he who always shunned these death traps, as he calls them—he feels safe. All his problems seem to fly away: Mrs. Suarez, the murder accusation, and even that business about the retirement home.

Only the situation with Mrs. Claudel remains tricky. Ferdinand is much too ashamed about it. He'll keep avoiding her and spending his free time with Juliette instead—if her father agrees, of course. Just then, a face peeks into the room.

"Oh, my child, I'm so happy to see you. We have to talk about that retirement home business again. Believe me, I don't need it!"

"Um, Ferdinand, it's Juliette, not Marion. I brought you things to eat." Her arms are full, not with flowers, but with irresistible goodies, including caramels (provided he hasn't lost his teeth), licorice, candied chestnuts, and nougat.

"Oh, pardon me, little one, where was my head? It's nice of you to come, but I don't want you to have any problems with your father because of me."

"Don't worry, Ferdinand, I talked to him. He still doesn't like you—you didn't do much to smooth things out—but he's willing to try for a fresh start. Our lunches aren't guaranteed, but this is something. It'd be too bad not to come over to eat anymore, especially since it's so much better than the cafeteria."

"But I don't know how to make much. I just made you some sauce dishes here, some pies there. Meanwhile, there was nothing in the fridge. My wife, now she was a veritable Cordon Bleu, and I encouraged her. 'It's not bad. Edible. You'll be able to make it again!'"

"You were always like that? I mean, never giving compliments?"

"I'm mischievous. And forthright. That you can't fault me on. Maybe people take my jokes as spitefulness if they don't know me, but I always tell the truth, even if it doesn't please everyone."

"Like a three-year-old?"

"Or ten! Don't you think? I've never known how to lie so people aren't hurt. I'm just like that, a man of truth. A straight shooter. I never cheated on my wife, for that matter."

"And you want a medal? My father never cheated on my mother, either!"

"That you know of. But fine . . . never mind. You're still a child. I don't know why we're talking about this anyway."

"You were telling me about how your wife reached the point of not being able to stand you anymore."

"Ah, yes, she didn't like the truth, she always took it personally. But it was objective feedback. And *I* didn't like questions with one right answer. What if she asked me, 'Is the skin on my neck sagging more than before?' How could I lie? 'No, my lovely, you're as firm as the day we met!' My body was drooping, too—she must have noticed it—so I wasn't going to tell tales. It would have broken the trust between us."

"So how would you answer?"

"'It's getting a little turkey neckish, a bit like the texture of tripe.'"

"I don't believe it! But why were you so . . . imaginative?"

"I don't know, it just came out. Sometimes, she wouldn't ask me anything but I couldn't keep myself from making comments. It was to help her, with constructive criticism. Sometimes, I didn't even need to say anything, she understood just looking at my face. For example, if she asked me what I thought of her new dress, I would tell her, 'No, that dress doesn't do anything for you. We can see your flabby arms and it gives you an awful belly. It looks like you're pregnant. Unless you are pregnant?'

"Once, she came back from the hairdresser with gray hair! She didn't ask for my thoughts, but at the same time she's a woman. A woman coming home from the hairdresser always looks for her husband's approval. But I said, 'Your silver hair isn't working! I know it's cheaper, but you look like a granny!'

"Then again, she nearly made me soil my pants over a pair of underwear. All I did was put them on her pillow without saying anything, so as not to order her around. But she got up on her high horse, saying, 'Do I look like a servant to you? You could have sent a telegram with: HOLE STOP MEND STOP URGENT STOP. It wouldn't have been worse!' How could I have guessed a mere pair of underpants could cause so much hassle? It's just she was good at sewing. She made Marion's clothes and little things for the house, like towels and tablecloths made out of the same red gingham, which I still can't stand the sight of!"

"Please, reassure me, did you love your wife?"

"Of course."

"Did you tell her?"

"No, not directly. That sort of effusiveness is always out of context. It bothers me. When she asked me squarely, 'Do you still love me?' like an ultimatum, I didn't answer with 'Of course, my dear,' even though it would have saved time and averted loads of arguments. I flat out couldn't. I didn't feel my heart ache like it did at the beginning, when we were young. So I answered with a joke, 'Bah, we get along, we're used to each other, we have our little routine, and frankly I'd be too lazy to look for better.' I never did have any luck with women!"

"What century are you living in, Ferdinand? No woman would tolerate even one percent of your actions or comments! Or else you'd have to pick somebody with amnesia. Tell me if you're interested, I know someone! Also, stop attributing everything to bad luck. Women leave you because you make them. Period! And you're not even capable of learning from your mistakes. Look how you're behaving with Mrs. Claudel. She's still reaching out to you. You can rectify the situation. Same with Marion. So do it! I *dream* of being able to relive my last conversation with my mother. I think about it a lot. I wasn't very nice to her at the end: I resented her for paying more attention to Emma. I resented her because I wasn't the only princess anymore. We're all a bit selfish. But not stupid! Did you ever do something, just once, just to make your wife happy?"

"No, but it's not so easy with women. You never know what they want. She did throw me a line once, though. She never stopped telling me, 'You know what my dream is? To travel abroad to see the Taj Mahal.' I didn't understand why she wanted to go to the other side of the world. I said, 'What for? You hate the heat! You panic when you see too many strangers all at once, you've never wanted to come camping with me in the mountains.' And when she bought an orange sari, I said she was ridiculous, that it wasn't carnival time."

"You're hopeless, Ferdinand. No offense, but *she* should've gotten a medal. How long did she stay with you?"

"From the age of eighteen to sixty-two. She told me she wasted her best years with me. Can you believe it? She has some nerve! Those aren't things you say during a divorce, especially when you're wrong."

"How was she wrong?"

"She cheated on me with the mailman and left me like an old sock! Even an old sock would have been treated better."

"Are you sure you want to tell me the rest? You seem tired."

"I need to talk about it, just once, and after that, it'll be forgotten. Even Marion—I've never told her what I did."

"You're scaring me, Ferdinand. You're not a serial killer after all, are you?"

"No, but I've done things I'm not proud of, things that pushed me past the point of no return. One day, when Louise wasn't home, I got into the house. Well, *her* house. I'd kept a set of keys she didn't know about. In there, I destroyed everything. I doused her daffodils with weed killer. Can you imagine? I've always hated postal service yellow, but that was too much. It was like she wanted to expose her adultery to the whole village. I was cuckolded, and by the mailman! I scratched up his car and punctured the tires. I cut the cords on all the household appliances. I even put nettles in her rain boots. Worse, I let the chickens out. They surely didn't get very far, with the neighbor's dogs and the foxes in the woods.

"When she came home, I hid and watched her burst into tears. That should have moved me, but I felt nothing. She deserved it! After that, she never let me come close to her and they moved to the south of France. All I know is she died from a stupid fall getting out of the bathtub. I can't say whether God punished her, because if there were any justice, I'd have been the first to pay the price. They say tough guys are the last to go. So there it is, the whole story."

"You put nettles in your wife's boots, and hoped she'd come back to you? Don't you have some regrets?"

"To be honest, yes, I have regrets, but if I could do it all over again, I don't think I'd do anything differently. The only difference is I'd wait every day for her to leave me, and when the moment came, I wouldn't be surprised. I'd have regrets for myself, but not for us. For me, for having failed again, for being incapable of positively influencing the course of my life. Those are my regrets. Not what you were expecting, eh?"

"But it's not over! You still have your daughter and your grandson. Maybe there are things you'd like to change with them."

"It's too late. I should've done it differently with my daughter, maybe taken her to the beach. Kids like the beach, don't they? Now they're on the other side of the world. Marion is always asking me to visit, but I've got nothing to do down there. She even wants to pay for my ticket, more than four hundred euros. Can you believe it? But it's out of the question. She'll work the whole time, I know it. And my grandson, I must have seen him fewer than ten times since he was born. He's seventeen now, and we'd have nothing to say to each other. And then, I'm not fond of going abroad. So, better to save ourselves the money and the trip."

"Yes, better to save yourself from life. Let's scrimp and save our money, and our feelings, too, for that matter," says Juliette.

Chapter Thirty-Four

Heavens to Betsy

Juliette returns the next day. The discussion from the previous day has been erased, just like the doctor's promise that Ferdinand would be discharged in the morning. It seems the old man has been forgotten yet again. Ferdinand is out of sorts. He no longer knows whether he dreamed that tirade, confessing his shameful misconduct. Of course he did. Otherwise, why would the little girl have come back?

They're in the middle of chatting, when an electronic noise resounds through the room, repeating several times. Ferdinand looks around for the source, wondering what he could have done now. That's when Juliette removes a touch screen tablet from her bag.

"I think your daughter would like to tell you something. You have things to say to each other, don't you?"

Juliette hands the device to Ferdinand, who feels like a chicken looking at a knife: dubious. He shoots a desperate look at Juliette, who turns the screen toward him. The old man then sees his daughter's face. Marion, still so far away, seems like she's right next to him. He can even detect signs of anxiety and fatigue.

"Hello, Papa."

"How does this thingamabob work? Where's the mic? Can she see me? I'm shaking too much, she's going to get seasick! Can you turn the sound up? I can't hear a thing. *Marion? Can you hear me?*"

"Yes, Papa, very well. You don't have to shout. Talk like you're on a telephone, no louder. How are you doing?"

"OK. I'm at the hospital but I've had it worse. It's weird to talk into this thing. You're fuzzy, Marion. Ah, the picture's better now! I can't wait to get out."

"I blame myself, especially for having missed your call. That dragged things out at the police station. You wouldn't look like that if I'd gotten your message immediately. It's my fault, but mostly Eric's. I called him to ask for an explanation. If I ever get my hands on him!"

"If I may, you're not looking too hot, either. Are you sleeping at night?"

"Not much at the moment. Between your umpteenth stay at the hospital and Alexandre getting health screenings . . ."

"What's wrong with Alexandre?"

"They don't really know yet, so no use worrying about it, which is easier said than done. You know me—I can get nervous and anxious over nothing. Right now, I can't sleep and I throw up everything I swallow."

"Let me know if there's anything I can do."

"That's nice, Papa. And I'm sorry about that retirement home business. I was really scared of losing you, especially after Mama's death. You're my remaining family, whether you like it or not. But I was wrong."

"That's OK, Marion. It's nothing. Besides, it didn't do me any harm to clean up. My slippers slide much better now. The hardest part was dealing with Mrs. Suarez."

"Papa, I've been doing a lot of thinking. The retirement home isn't the solution. Something changed in you a while ago. Just offering your help with Alexandre proves it. But I still can't help but worry. You spend your days alone, with nothing to do. Have you thought about getting another dog? I wasn't in favor of it at first, but now I think it would do you good."

"I don't need a dog. I don't feel like starting all over again with the training. Then the feelings . . . Just to see it die before me again. And I have Juliette now. It's kind of the same, a stomach on legs, minus the walks. She's a nice little girl."

"But that pains me, too. You're going to wind up knowing a stranger better than your own grandson. He needs his grandfather."

"I'm not the one who chose to live in Singapore."

Ferdinand has a gift for setting fires—not just where there's fuel, but also where there's a peace pipe.

"Papa, it was to get away from you and Mama! You put me in the middle of your fights. I couldn't see either of you without hearing your complaints. Worse, all your 'Talk to him! He'll listen to *you*' or 'Go see her and ask her to come back. I'm ready to accept her apology.' It's sad to say, but with Mama's death, at least it's calmed down. And I've changed, too. I'm getting older and I'm realizing what's really important. In one year, I almost lost you twice. That's not a life—not for you, not for me, not for Alex."

Marion takes a deep breath and continues.

"I've made a big decision, Papa. I'm selling the apartment in the complex and I'd like you to come live with us in Singapore. What do you think?"

"Darling, I'm not sure I heard right. It cut out. Anyway, I have to hang up now. The nurse just came in and it's time for my treatment. Love you!"

"Papa, don't hang up. Did you hear my proposal?"

For several long seconds, both of them are silent. Ferdinand's face remains shut down, then he finally blurts out, "I think so, yes."

"I'm aware that means an enormous change. But it's family! I'm not asking for an immediate response, I'm not forcing you into anything. I'm just saying I'd like it. OK, I'll leave you to your nurses. Call me as soon as you get home and we'll talk about it some more. Hugs, Papa. I love you."

"Go on, Marion. Bye. How do you turn this thingamabob off, Juliette?"

Chapter Thirty-Five
All Fun and Games 'til Someone Gets Hurt

Ferdinand has been back at home for two days. His convalescence at the hospital was longer than anticipated, and he's relieved to see his apartment again. As Marion asked him to do, he informed her of his return home, while trying to break the record for shortest phone conversation: eleven seconds. He didn't want to give her a chance to reopen the discussion about the proposed move. Ferdinand hates moving, and he can't seriously entertain his daughter's request.

For two days, he's lived as a recluse: neither Juliette nor Beatrice knows he's back. He wants to be forgotten, and to take advantage of his solitude to do some thinking. Furthermore, his relationship with Beatrice is still stuck in his craw. First, she flirts with him by telling him about her life and sharing her feelings. Then she sends him packing. Then she rescues him from an unjust conviction at the eleventh hour, only to force him back into the hospital, where he hates the green walls and incessant beeping that indicates life and death. Not to mention the car ride, when she nearly killed him. What a nut!

OK, sometimes he thinks he's a little loony, too. But above all he has his pride. How can he spend time with her again? Where would they begin? A tongue-lashing? Excuses? A kiss? He decides to avoid her, along with the evening's bridge party.

The plastic clock displays 5:52. Ferdinand paces around. The closer it gets to the top of the hour, the more anxious he gets. He reassesses each conversation with Beatrice, looks out the window as if the solution to his predicament is there, then checks the time again.

5:53. *In seven minutes, Beatrice will come to my door to beg me to come play. But I won't go. I won't!* It's not that he blames her. He knew deep down what she would say. Eighty years of experience taught him that. *It's always the same with women. They ask me to love them, then toss me aside when I finally have feelings! I won't go play tonight, that's for sure! In any case, she won't have to ring the bell—the bridge set is sitting on her doormat. She'll get the message.* 5:54. *This clock isn't working. It's slow! And it's on Beatrice's side—it's slowly torturing me.*

5:56. Ferdinand sighs. He looks through the peephole and sees the bridge set is still where he left it. Beatrice should discover it soon. *I'd like to see her face when she realizes I'm not coming. That it's over between us.* Ferdinand, like a caged animal, returns to his station in front of the window, staring into space. *Then again, it would be a shame to leave the complex now. The concierge isn't here anymore to bother me, the neighbor ladies make eyes at me, Juliette brings me licorice . . .*

The doorbell rings. *But it's only 5:57. Beatrice is getting rude, she's early! Anyway, I'm not here.* Silence. Ferdinand presses himself against the wall. He ceases moving, holds his breath. Then, he remembers. *Darn, the light. I should have turned it off. Now she'll see it shining underneath the door.* Stealthily, Ferdinand shuffles in his slippers to the light switch in the entryway. He's turning blue in the face. He presses it, and the light goes out. Whew!

But the desire to see his neighbor's pleading face is too strong. He lifts the cover on the peephole, adjusts his lens, and sticks his eye in. Nothing! Suddenly a worried little voice calls, "Yoo-hoo, is anyone there? Where is that damned light? Yoo-hoo . . ."

It's not Beatrice's voice . . . the bell rings again . . .

All of a sudden, the light turns back on. A white shape appears. Tall. Blond. Slender. From the back. A woman, in a long white fur coat. She turns around and scrutinizes the door, as if she were trying to see through it. Ferdinand can almost feel the heat of her gaze piercing him. He concentrates and makes out the woman's features more clearly. Blue-gray eyes, a plump face little ravaged by the years, a delicate mouth redrawn in red. A beautiful woman, sixty-five at the most. Ferdinand has never seen her around here, otherwise he would have noticed her, maybe even tried to talk to her! Suddenly the white shape seems to dart toward him. *Shoot.* Ferdinand closes his eyes and mouth as tightly as possible, as if to disappear. *She saw me.*

The stranger rings again. "Hello. Is anyone there? I'm a bit late. I got lost in the stairwell and there are no numbers on the floors. I'm here for the bridge party." Ferdinand exhales to empty his lungs entirely. *Whew! She's not looking for me.* Ferdinand opens the door and sticks his head out.

"It's the door across the way, little lady. You'll see, I put the bridge set on the doorstep."

"Oh, thank you! Yes, the game, how silly of me. Where was my head? I'm sorry to have bothered you." She takes a deep breath, her hands trembling. "May I ask you to lend me your arm to help me across? My legs don't carry me well anymore. I was really frightened in the dark . . ."

"Uh, yes, I'll help you. Uh . . . there's been a misunderstanding . . ." Ferdinand takes his keys and pulls the door shut behind him.

"Thank you so much, sir, for your help. I'm lucky to have found a knight in shining armor. Isn't that wonderful. I get the wrong door and stumble upon a charming man who plays bridge, no less. May I know whom I have the honor of speaking to? I'm Madeleine," she says, catching the old man's arm.

Ferdinand's head is spinning. He's the one who needs to hold on. He's bowled over. He'd been planning to play dead all evening, but now finds himself on the landing approaching Beatrice's door-bell, with a seductive woman on his arm. How can he flee before being spotted by his neighbor, while still leaving a good impression on the lovely Madeleine?

But the door opens to reveal Beatrice. "Ah, I thought I'd heard your door. I'm *truly* delighted you've come, Ferdinand. I see you've already met Madeleine, your new partner. She's the most seasoned player I know. Come in, come in. You like winning, Ferdinand, so here's someone your speed. Besides, you've surely heard Juliette talk about Madeleine. She's her grandmother!"

Madeleine lights up. "How nice to find out I'm on the arm of Mr. Ferdinand. I'm thrilled! We'll see each other regularly then. I'll be living upstairs from now on. At least, I think so. My memory plays tricks on me sometimes."

The game has four players as soon as Mr. Palisson arrives, who helps Ferdinand unfold the bridge table. He explains the rules three times. Nevertheless, everyone has a lovely time, and Beatrice enjoys the presence of her neighbor. Madeleine has the most entertaining evening she's had in months. At least, as far as she can remember. As for Ferdinand, he wins, but doesn't even think to enjoy his victory, he's so turned upside down by the superb woman who spends the evening touching his arm . . .

Chapter Thirty-Six

Once and for All

The Christmas season is approaching. Beatrice will spend ten days with her children, then she'll celebrate New Year's Eve at the retirement home with her sister-in-law. Juliette is leaving for Normandy with her father, little sister, and grandmother, where Madeleine will take a spa cure. Like every year, Ferdinand has nothing planned. Marion doesn't get any vacation time, and Alexandre will spend his time off with his father, as he does every year. And that's it! Ferdinand's made the rounds of all his options. He'll be alone. Like last year. Except last year, there was Daisy.

It's the last day of school before vacation, and Juliette has promised to have lunch with Ferdinand. He's prepared her favorite dish: chicken and pasta shells au jus and pickles. For dessert, he's planned a surprise: a homemade chocolate mousse. A first! The only spoonful he's allowed himself was delicious.

The table is set, when the little girl, punctual as always, tumbles through the door. She takes a report out of her school bag and shows it to him. He never had grades like those. This little girl will go far. Ferdinand is proud of her. Juliette sits at the table, a chatterbox as usual. The chicken isn't quite cooked yet. She tells him about her morning at school. By way of an appetizer, she gorges on the pickles.

Suddenly all the lights go out. The fridge and the oven, too. A power failure. A quick check through the peephole reveals there's light in the stairwell. Ferdinand resets the breaker. The power doesn't come back on. Blast! His Christmas dinner will be ruined if the chicken is raw and the mousse warm. Seized by an impulse, he rushes out and rings Beatrice's doorbell. Surprised, pencil in hand, she opens the door, all smiles.

"Hello, Ferdinand. How's it going?"

Juliette sticks her head out onto the landing and waves to the nonagenarian.

"Ah, I see you have a visitor. Hello, Juliette! Can I do something for you, Ferdinand?"

"Beatrice, I have a favor to ask you. There's been a power outage at my place and the breaker isn't cooperating. While we wait, there's an emergency: I need to finish cooking the chicken in your oven, if that won't be a bother."

Beatrice smiles. "I love chicken. But living all alone, I end up eating it all week . . ."

Ferdinand gets the message immediately. Beatrice is smart—she's always known how to communicate her desires tactfully.

"Will you do us the honor of joining us, Beatrice?"

"What a wonderfully kind gesture! With great pleasure. And it was so nicely proposed. Let's not bother with going back and forth from one kitchen to the other. Let's eat in my dining room."

The clock is ticking, and Ferdinand doesn't have time to refuse. He agrees. Juliette has followed the conversation and already gathered everything up. The chicken, the pasta, and the mousse, like a procession of offerings, leave Ferdinand's apartment and cross the hall to take their places in Beatrice's kitchen. In the dining room, the white tablecloth is already spread out with nary a wrinkle. The table is set and the pitcher filled with water. A fat loaf of farmhouse bread is on a cutting board. Ferdinand hadn't thought of bread, even though, according to Juliette, there's nothing better for adding zest.

Once the chicken's in the oven, Ferdinand takes his place at the head of the table. To his left is Beatrice, and to his right, Juliette. The old man returns to the oven to supervise the fowl. From the kitchen, he hears the conversation flowing easily between the old lady and the little girl. They're discussing literature. Mrs. Claudel seems surprised to learn that this little girl has been doing entirely inappropriate reading.

"No wonder your classmates find you strange," he hears Beatrice say. "I know just the right book to help you impress the kids at recess!" She fetches a tome from her library.

"You're too young to read such an enormous book, but when you feel like it, or have the courage, it's one of the best in existence.

The Fellowship of the Ring by Tolkien. It's a classic, and I'm giving it to you."

Ferdinand returns with the steaming platter. His eyes widen at the thick volume Juliette is looking at. Some present! Then he changes his mind upon reading the title. Even he's heard of it. Juliette will give him the lowdown.

"Ferdinand," begins Beatrice, "you'll be happy to learn that Commissioner Balard has been censured for the poor treatment he inflicted on you. I was right: your health was in pitiful condition. According to the tests, it's mostly the stress that mauled your heart. Do you have cardiac problems?"

Ferdinand smiles. His heart has indeed been mauled over these past few months. And it's not about to stop . . . Beatrice continues on about the commissioner, whom she cannot stand. Juliette, on the other hand, loads up her plate.

"This sauce is so good, Ferdinand. Bravo!"

"Wait 'til you taste dessert. I think you'll like that, too." After their meal, he asks, "Can I take your plates?"

Ferdinand leaves the table with an armload and comes back with a bowl covered in aluminum foil. When he uncovers the chocolate mousse, Juliette's eyes light up.

"I love chocolate mousse! How did you know?"

"Little Miss Know-It-All isn't the only one who knows everything! I have my sources."

"Gramma Maddie, I'll bet. Is it her recipe?"

Juliette gulps down spoonful after spoonful, to Beatrice's astonishment.

"This child has an appetite! She would eat you out of house and home. I'm kidding, my dear. But you certainly do know how to wield a fork."

"I've gotta run," Juliette says. "I'm going to give you a kiss, Ferdinand, because I won't see you before we leave for Normandy. We're heading out first thing tomorrow morning. Thanks again for the book, Beatrice. I'll tell you if I like it. Merry Christmas to you both!"

"It was a pleasure to get to know you better, Juliette. If you like the book, the next one's waiting for you. Have a wonderful holiday with your family and give Madeleine my regards. I hope we meet another time, for another lunch . . ."

Ferdinand accompanies Juliette out and helps her hoist her school bag onto her shoulders. He notices how much the little girl's grown in just a few months and already he can't wait to see her again after the holidays. Then the old man, a bit embarrassed, musters his courage.

"Juliette, can I ask you a favor? Can you give this little something to Madeleine from me, for Christmas? It's really nothing, but I know she'll like it. Have a great holiday. We'll see each other when you get back."

Juliette disappears, and Ferdinand goes back to Beatrice's. Their conversation picks back up in the same lighthearted tone. They talk about coffee and television shows to watch together.

On the landing, the light's gone out again. But no one could guess that the breaker was intentionally thrown by Beatrice.

***

After lunch, the two neighbors settle in on Beatrice's sofa to drink their cups of coffee. Ferdinand is ill at ease about this unforeseen tête-à-tête. Will he still be able to be friends with her after his stupid declaration? He doubts it, but he appreciates Beatrice's company—she never judges him.

Awkwardly, he says, "I know I'm late getting around to it, but I want to thank you for everything you've done for me. Coming to get me at the police station, bringing me to the hospital . . . You didn't have to do it. It really touched me, especially after my . . . declaration, which must have made you uncomfortable."

"To say the least. At more than ninety years old, I'm out of the habit. But what I did was nothing, Ferdinand. It's what they call friendship. And you know, you were the simplest case of my career!"

"And the only one?" Ferdinand's smile is joined by Beatrice's.

"You should thank Juliette instead. That little girl is marvelous! She's the one who dug up Mrs. Suarez's prescription, and I prefer not to know where or how. She has very fixed ideas, a bit like you. According to her, the death of our late concierge is the fault of Mrs. Berger's cat, who was roaming the trash room, looking for a mouse. Juliette says Mrs. Suarez was frightened by the sight of its eyes shining in the darkness. That's what brought on the heart attack. A grim tale, in any event. Then again, it's been a beautiful year for our friendship! To think, without that threat of the retirement home, you might never have said a word to me.

And you wouldn't have met Juliette, either. That little girl loves you a lot, you know."

"Not too much, I hope. Because if that's the case, I'm afraid she'll be sad when she learns about my departure."

"Your departure? Good God! For where?"

"Singapore."

"Oh. That's so far! But it's your decision and I'm sure you've weighed the pros and cons. That's brave, Mr. Brun. If you leave, we're going to miss you enormously, Juliette and me."

"I don't have the slightest desire to leave my apartment or certain people, but Marion asked me to. She said, 'It's family,' and I think she's right . . ."

Chapter Thirty-Seven

Elementary, My Dear Watson

Stationed in front of his window in his armchair, Ferdinand contemplates the naked trees' coating of downy flakes. The sunlight plays on the ice crystals and makes the branches sparkle. It's Christmas Day. The previous evening, the old man stayed home and thought about Beatrice, who was celebrating with her grandchildren. Then he thought about Juliette, who doesn't believe in Santa Claus anymore, but who will certainly be happy when she returns to find that Ferdinand gave her a subscription to the magazine *The New Detective*, after her exploits in the resolution of the Suarez case. He can't wait to see her reaction.

Next, Ferdinand's thoughts turn to another woman: Madeleine. He thinks of her frail, childlike voice, which seems surprised at the most ordinary things; her mischievous laugh still resonating in his head; her intense gaze, looking for approval. And especially her hand, with its delicate skin, so soft, nonchalantly resting on his, just for a moment, yet an eternity. *Oh, Madeleine!*

Ferdinand dwells on the moments he's spent with her and invents snappier responses. He even imagines their future discussions. "They're playing a new movie at the cinema. Everyone has good things to say about it. Would you like to go see it?"

Ferdinand decides to take a walk to leave a few traces of human presence in the deserted, immaculate streets. He puts on his overcoat, wraps himself up in a scarf, and tugs his beret down over his ears. Upon opening the door, he discovers a little package on the doorstep. A letter with no postmark. The old man goes back inside, closes the door, and leans against it. The handwriting is loopy and familiar. He smiles and eagerly opens the envelope, pulling out a sheet of narrowly lined paper.

My dearest Ferdinand,

I'm writing to you because I know you're alone at Christmas and I wanted you to know I'm thinking about you. This year was very difficult for you. The tragic loss of Daisy, the bus accident, the threat of the retirement home, the disputes with the neighbors, Mrs. Suarez's inspections, the arrest, your stays in the hospital. A hard year, but rich in emotion. With very nice meetings, as well. I'm thinking about ours, of course. It would have taken very little for you to leave me hanging around on your doorstep! Fortunately I thought of the licorice.

I'm also thinking of Beatrice, that supergranny who lives five yards away from you and who you'd never even spoken to, except maybe with a grunt. Look how your experiences have brought you together today, and all you'll share from now on.

Finally, I'm thinking of Gramma Maddie. Maybe I'm wrong, but I get the impression she didn't leave you cold. And I even think I saw a little gleam in your eyes that wasn't there a few months ago. Desire. The desire not to be alone anymore, the desire to love again, the desire to really start living.

I'm going on and on but I'm forgetting the most important thing: I have to thank you for the subscription to New Detective *(I'd be a terrible investigator if I wasn't capable of figuring out my Christmas presents in advance). Our daily lunches should give us time to shed light on the darkest mysteries. I have a little something for you, too. Go out onto your landing. Look, there's a bigger box. Open it . . .*

Ferdinand is positive there wasn't a box next to the letter, otherwise he would have started by opening it. He opens the door, and there, indeed, is a cardboard box of considerable size, the sort that holds a . . . vacuum cleaner. Or a microwave oven. *Oh, that cheeky monkey! Is she trying to send me a message?* Ferdinand tears off the wrapping paper and uncovers a box for . . . a scanner-printer! Huh? Ferdinand doesn't even have a computer. Perplexed, he goes back to reading.

> *So, what do you think? I hope you're happy.*
> *I was a little afraid of your reaction. Then again,*
> *I won't be there for two weeks, so you'll have time*
> *to get used to him and stop holding it against me.*
> *Most of all, don't leave him in the box. I'm sure*
> *you'll know how to find a spot for him . . .*

Ferdinand stops his reading cold. He swears he heard a noise close by. A groan, not a whimper. *Oh, no! Not another accident. I'm alone. They're going to accuse me again!* Then suddenly, he understands. *I'm so stupid! Why didn't I think of it sooner? Quick!* Ferdinand grabs the box, finds little holes in it, separates the side panels, and out pops a tiny brown head, furry and splotched with white. Ferdinand gently lifts the animal, who turns out to be impossibly light. A tiny little puppy! The first contact is warm. Soft. The eyes are wet and sleepy. Ferdinand cradles the puppy against his chest. Under his fingers he feels the rapid beating of its heart, which gradually slows with his caresses. "Everything's all right. Don't be afraid, I'm here."

Ferdinand doesn't dare move, for fear of disturbing the puppy and this peaceful moment. Everything's OK. He's not alone anymore. Then, he remembers that he interrupted his reading before the end. Gently, he retrieves the letter from his pocket. The puppy has already fallen asleep.

> *. . . I'm sure you'll know how to find a spot for him, close to your heart. My father found him along with his three brothers near a construction site. They were hidden in a box soaked by the rain. But the veterinarian said he was in good health, that he just needed love and comfort. Like you! Take good care of Sherlock. Yes, the little beagle is a male. Now we have to make you love men: your grandson, Alexandre, and my father, for starters. I'll help you. Also think about buying more pickles. I finished the jar . . . There, the car is going to leave so I have to stop. Big hugs. See you soon.*

> *Juliette*

> *PS I don't know what you did to her, but Gramma Maddie won't talk about anything but you. She's on a loop: "But why didn't Ferdinand come with us? It's not nice to have left him all alone! Antoine?"*

Ferdinand's heart starts to beat faster. The puppy whimpers, and Ferdinand calms him with a reassuring caress. The letter slips to the floor. He smiles. Life seems sweeter.

Chapter Thirty-Eight

Yellow Bellied

Ferdinand is waiting by his telephone. Marion is supposed to call any minute. He's agreeing to come live with her in Singapore, and he's extremely nervous about announcing his decision. Marion must be hoping for it without daring to believe in it. They'd set the time, and his daughter is already ten minutes late. If the minutes continue to tick by, he's afraid he'll crack and change his mind.

It's 4:30 p.m., and still nothing. Ferdinand checks the dial tone, hangs up. 4:31. Finally, it rings. Maybe his telephone was left off the hook, after all, and Marion has been trying to reach him for thirty minutes.

"Hello, Marion?"

"Uh, no, this is Tony."

"Tony? I don't know any Tony. Sorry, but I have to hang up, I'm waiting for a very important call. Good-bye."

"Wait, yes, I know. You're waiting for a call from Marion. She asked me to call you."

"What's that? Why can't Marion call me herself? What's going on? Did something happen to her? And who are *you*?"

"Marion's in the hospital with Alexandre. The doctors just made the diagnosis. It's renal failure."

"What are you talking about? Is this a joke? They must have made a mistake. He's seventeen years old . . . And where's Marion? Why can't she tell me herself?"

"Marion is taking some tests to see if she's compatible with Alexandre. He needs a kidney transplant."

"But who are you? Are you a doctor?"

"No, I'm not a doctor. You know me, I think. I'm Tony Gallica. The mailman . . ."

"The mailman? I don't know any mailman. Not mine, not my daughter's. Wait . . . you're the swine who ran off with my wife!"

"I wouldn't have put it like that, but yes . . . Louise's companion."

"What are you doing mixed up in this family affair? Why is Marion asking you to call me?"

"I came to Singapore for Christmas, like every other year. The results came back during my visit, and I decided to stay. They need me and nothing's keeping me in France anyway."

"Oh, no! This is not starting again! This is not happening like that! Tell Marion I'm coming on the next flight. And give me the hospital address so I know where to go, for Pete's sake!" Tony gives it to him. Ferdinand starts to hang up, then adds, "Tell me, Tony. I have two questions for you. First, do you believe Louise was happy afterward? I mean, well . . ."

"I'm not going to express an opinion about your relationship, but she told me that with me she finally felt beautiful, alive. More womanly, too. She was more serene and radiant than ever on our last trip to India. It was her dream, you know. She spent hours gazing at the Taj Mahal. And then you know about her tragic end that cut our story short, her fall in the bathroom at our hotel in Singapore, while we were visiting Marion on the way back. You wanted to ask me something else . . ."

"Yes. It's not so much a question . . . just leave me and my family alone! Get out of our lives. I don't want to deal with you again!"

"We'll let Marion decide. I watched Alexandre grow up and I've spent much more time with him than you have. He's like my grandson. I can't abandon him while he's going through the most difficult time in his life. He needs all the love he can get. Goodbye, Ferdinand. We'll see each other in a few days in Singapore."

Ferdinand hangs up, devastated. He doesn't even realize what he just heard: the flesh of his flesh, sick? And that swine who's taking his place, who already stole his wife from him—he won't steal his daughter, or his grandson, too! They're *his* family.

Chapter Thirty-Nine
Travel Broadens the Mind

Yes, family is important, but what worries they cause! Ferdinand was much calmer before he cared about others. Ever since learning the terrible news about Alexandre, he's been out of sorts. He even has trouble being good company for little Juliette, who calls him to find out how he's doing, and to make sure he indeed found his present. He doesn't want the conversation to drag, but his heart is heavy.

"What's more important, Juliette? The decision you make or the reason for your decision?"

"Well . . . I don't know. Why are you asking me that? Are you turning into a philosopher? Who cares, right?"

"I don't have the heart to laugh, little one, I'm sorry. I'm burnt out."

"Again? But what's going on?"

"I don't want to bother you with my business, but to make a long story short, my grandson is experiencing renal failure and has to be operated on right away. I'm moving to Singapore. I think I made the decision mostly because the mailman is there, playing replacement grandpa. It annoys me to compete at a time like this! I have to pack my bags, my flight leaves tomorrow. I'm not sure we'll see each other again very soon."

"Oh, no! I don't want to lose you. I'm sad for Alexandre and I hope he gets better as quick as possible, but I didn't think I'd ever see you move, let alone so soon."

"I didn't think I'd move abroad one day, either, let alone for good. But in any case, I feel like I'm doing something, even if deep down I feel completely powerless. It's horrible, that lump in your gut when someone close to you is sick. It's so unfair. I'm an old hypochondriac—sickness should have come looking for *me*! I'm going to be good for something or someone, for once in my life!"

"But it doesn't work like that. I can't believe you're leaving . . . And Gramma Maddie . . . She's going to be so sad. Isn't there the slightest chance you'll stay? No . . . forget what I just said. Leave, it's the best thing to do. I'll think about you when I'm eating the nasty stuff the cafeteria serves, and also when I see Matteo lower his eyes when he sees me coming. You'll be taking your puppy at least? So you'll think about me sometimes?"

"Yes, of course. It's not going to be practical, but I think an animal could be fun for Alexandre."

"OK, and you'll Skype me, now that you know how."

"Do you think I'm Beatrice? Yes, I'll try, Juliette. Every week. You'll have to see Sherlock grow up, since you're kind of his mummy, too."

Chapter Forty

The Die Is Cast

Ferdinand is worrying himself sick. Too much change. Too many things pushing him beyond his comfort zone. He only wanted to live quietly, waiting for death to find his address. Even Dr. Labrousse had told him, "No emotional shocks." He's had plenty! Plagued by doubt while facing the immensity of his task, the old man decides to draw up a list:

1. *Pack my suitcase.*
   But what to do with Sherlock?
2. *Get on the plane (for the first time).*
   Everybody takes planes. There's almost never an accident. But Ferdinand has a bad premonition. Note for later: check which airline Marion picked. Then again, it's too late to change. This is starting out well!

3. *Go to a foreign country.*

This seems insurmountable because he speaks only French. Furthermore, he has a terrible sense of direction. As for telling the difference between the various natives . . .

4. *Make arrangements to move out belongings.*
Horror, horror, horror!

5. *Move in.*

Definitively. And to a place he doesn't know, to live off his daughter, probably in a ridiculously small room, where he's going to lose all autonomy. Back to square one: a kind of retirement home!

6. *Confront my hypochondria.*

For the first time in his life, see illness up close, real illness, the kind that can take your life. And unflinchingly endure the wait for a potential donor, daily visits to the hospital. Come each day with an even temper and courage to share.

7. *Confront the mailman.*

The illegitimate grandfather off the back bench, the Latin Lover of the postal service who stole his wife.

There! Ferdinand decides to stop his list here and tackle the tasks, one by one. First, the suitcase. Despite the heaps of clothes scattered all around, the suitcase just stays empty. Sherlock, head tilted, tries to understand his master's game: are you supposed to put things in or take things out of the suitcase?

Ferdinand would like to stop time, or, rather, go back to the moment he left the jail. The moment the threat of the retirement home went away, the moment he didn't have to choose between France and Singapore, the moment his grandson wasn't sick, the moment before he knew Tony as a real person.

No, this isn't the time to hold a grudge or rewrite the past. Ferdinand has to concentrate on the future. *Come on, pull yourself together.* He still has an hour to pack his suitcase before leaving for the airport. Finally, the old man decides to take everything. He struggles with the zipper on his bag and manages to close it by sitting on it. In less than five minutes, the taxi will buzz at his intercom. Sherlock, intrigued, looks at his master, all ready to go.

Ferdinand pulls on his overcoat, puts on his beret, and sits down on his suitcase. He looks at his apartment, scrutinizes every detail to bring the memories with him, reassuring, familiar. Over there, it'll be the unknown, communal life, crowded in with Marion, crowded in a little hospital room, surrounded by strangers. Not to mention Marion, who'll be—deservedly—stressed, but his presence may be even more stressful for her, considering how she frets over and infantilizes him. The more he thinks about it, the more Ferdinand has his doubts. What if he ran away? Run away, yes. Somewhere they'll leave him be, without phone calls (damned telephone just rang, and he unplugged it), without doorbells bothering him . . . Absorbed in his new plans, Ferdinand is suddenly interrupted by the doorbell! *Grrr . . . It can't be true! Every time it's Beatrice and she's going to make me late. That is, if I do leave.* Ferdinand decides to go open the door, takes a glance through the peephole, and discovers, dumbfounded, Eric. He opens the door and takes out his suitcase.

"What do you want? You've come at a bad time. I'm going away. So if you don't have a search warrant, you can get out of here."

"I know what you're doing and I've come to stop you."

"Again? You're a broken record, Super Cop."

"I've come to tell you it's not worth catching your flight. Right now, Marion and Alexandre are on a plane and they're landing at Roissy in two hours. And if you listened to what people tell you over the phone instead of hanging up, we'd all save some time!"

"What are you talking about? I heard from Marion. Well, not exactly Marion—she was at the hospital in Singapore with Alexandre. They're waiting for me. So I don't understand why they'd change their plans without telling me."

"Marion thinks the care will be better here. I don't know if she's right. In any case, she's wanted to come back to France for a while, and now she has a good reason to chuck everything. She wants to be sure she understands the subtleties of the procedure and the treatments. And Alexandre needs to be surrounded by his family, and by two potential transplant donors, you and me!"

"Marion said that?"

"No, but it's the least I can do for Alexandre, don't you think? Fine, it's not everything, but I mostly came to ask you to prepare their rooms. After thirteen hours in flight, they're going to need to rest. I would've invited them to my place, but my studio is too small. I'm off to pick them up from the airport. See you later. No hard feelings about last time?"

Ferdinand closes the door on his ex-son-in-law, shakes his head, and pinches himself . . . Ow! No, he's not dreaming. His family is coming. And staying with him. In less than three hours! His heart races with joy, stress, excitement. He waves his arms, hopping around in an unlikely dance. Sherlock isn't sure he understands it all, but he yelps as feverishly as his master. The old man tries to recover his senses and ends up seizing his pen to draw up a new list, longer than the first one:

1. *Prove that blood ties are stronger than anything.*
    Stronger than fear, especially. And the mailman! Even though he doesn't know Ferdinand well, Alexandre needs him, needs his presence and maybe also his kidney. That'll be what differentiates him from Tony. Blood ties. Yes, he loves Alexandre, but he can't lie: that thing about the transplant scares him stiff.

2. *Resolve to give up my peaceful existence.*
    And try to be happy about it.

3. *Make room in my house.*
    To welcome two people, plus Sherlock.

4. *Support Alexandre on a daily basis.*
    With the difficulties of treatment, setting aside his fear of medications, hospitals, sick people who vomit and cough . . .

5. *Put up with my enemies.*
    Super Cop, for one. The mailman, for another, if he has the misfortune to show himself.

6. *Shake up my habits.*

    His lunches with Juliette, his coffees with Beatrice, his future meetings with Madeleine . . . *Oh, Madeleine!*

7. *Leave room for the unexpected.*

    For good and less-good news. Accept change, don't fight against it.

8. *Change my epitaph.*

    All things considered, "Alone at last" is perhaps a bit exaggerated. A little interaction can't hurt.

Ferdinand starts to realize he might be able to stay in his home. For good. He doesn't dare believe it yet. He's never had any luck, or respite, or happy endings. There's going to be a ring, either at the door or the telephone. Probably someone he hates, Tony or Eric, the ghost of Mrs. Suarez or Louise. Like a cruel reminder of the reality of his life, and which will definitively remove all hope of happiness.

But nothing happens. No ringing, no telephone call, no doorbell. Sherlock plays quietly in his basket. Suddenly, however, he gets excited. The puppy heads for the door, furiously wagging his tail. There's someone in the stairwell. It can't be Beatrice, she's with her family. Nor Juliette. Marion and Alexandre are still on the plane, and Eric is heading for the airport. The old man is practically alone in the complex. Whatever happens, he'll ignore whoever wants to bring him the next piece of news that will once more change the course of his life. Sherlock yaps noisily, and Ferdinand shoots daggers at him. The bell rings.

"What now?"

Chapter Forty-One

Two of a Kind

Ferdinand musters all his courage and opens the door. He finds a familiar face, smiling.

"Well, hello, Mr. Brun. I have your mail. A letter from Normandy, notably."

Mr. Suarez, even shorter than his wife, happily discovers the playful pup nibbling at his shoes and strokes him tenderly in return.

"Ah, I see you've gotten another dog. You did the right thing! I liked your Daisy so much. I shouldn't be telling you that, my wife must be spinning in her grave . . . It's just that it was a difficult year for us. You can't always choose what happens to you. I've finished my rounds, and you're the only one who isn't away for the holidays. How'd you like to make the most of the sunshine and drink a little port in the courtyard? It's a bit brisk but we can introduce Rocco and . . ."

"Sherlock. Well, I won't say no. I really need it. I just had an emotional week and it's not about to stop. Because the dog is one thing, but I just learned the family's coming. My daughter and her son. If you only knew! My poor grandson . . ."

"Oh, I forgot, I also have this for you." Mr. Suarez hands a little black book to Ferdinand. "My wife's book of grievances. There's a whole chapter about you. I don't have any use for it. Keep it or throw it out. I don't feel right about saving the thing."

The two men descend the thirteen steps leading to the courtyard. While Mr. Suarez goes back to his loge for Rocco, Ferdinand heads toward the trash area. For the first time he discovers there are simple explanations for the sorting. Paper: yellow bin. The last voyage of the little black book! In the distance, he hears canaries singing, ignoring the happy sounds of Rocco and Sherlock squabbling over a piece of kibble.

Mr. Suarez calls to Ferdinand, "You want a little slice of kings' cake?"

A bit of paper has just flown out of the black book and fallen at Ferdinand's feet. Proudly, he moves to put it in the appropriate bin, when suddenly a word attracts his attention. *Daisy*. Ferdinand freezes. He sets his glasses on his nose and reads, on what looks to be a business card: *Long-Term Kennel*. There's an address and a telephone number. Someone has hand-written the name of his dog. Ferdinand feels as though his heart will give out. A year, nearly a year since his dog died. Died and was cremated before his eyes. What can this scrap of paper change about that? He doesn't dare hope anything. Impossible to hold his legs back, he rushes over to Mr. Suarez, who's pointing to where Juliette's father should install a beehive for the complex. Ferdinand cuts him off.

"Do you know this kennel?"

Mr. Suarez grabs the card, holds it out to bring it into focus. "Yes, that's where we put Rocco when we go to Portugal in the summer. If my wife contacted the kennel when she was looking for Daisy, she'll surely have dealt with José," he adds, reading the dog's name on the card.

"Do you have one of those portable contraptions I can borrow?"

"My cell phone? Of course. These things are useful, especially for emergencies."

Ferdinand types frantically on the keys, but nothing happens. He gets annoyed.

"Wait, you didn't unlock it. I'll put the number in for you and when it starts ringing I'll hand it over." Mr. Suarez taps away on the screen and hands the phone to a feverish Ferdinand.

Ferdinand steps away when a woman's voice answers, "Long-Term Kennel, hello."

"Hello, ma'am. Would you happen to have in your kennel a female Great Dane, gray in color? Her name is Daisy."

"No, I don't think so. Are we watching her right now? I only joined the team last summer . . ."

"Could you ask José if he remembers my dog? A certain Mrs. Suarez would have asked him about keeping Daisy."

"Hang on. He's out with the dogs. I'll ask if that means anything to him. Stay on the line."

The woman leaves for two minutes and twenty seconds (that's what the cell phone says). Ferdinand jumps up and down. He's anxious and upset, hoping for something that can't be. Three minutes and forty seconds. This will cost Mr. Suarez, too. Ferdinand can't stand this torture anymore and is about to hang up, when the voice comes through again.

"All right, it's complicated. Yes, Mrs. Suarez inquired with us about a long-term stay for a female Great Dane. We did indeed keep her for several months, but we had to part with her."

Ferdinand remains speechless. "Several months." How is that possible? He saw her lifeless body. He cremated her. She didn't have her collar anymore and what remained wasn't pretty. But there was no doubt. You can't replace one dog with another so easily. Daisy was dead: how could she simultaneously be in a kennel? And if she was alive, what did "we had to part with her" mean?

"I'm not sure I understand. 'Part with her'? What do you mean by that, exactly?"

"According to what José told me, the Great Dane, Daisy, came to us at the beginning of spring. There weren't many dogs at the time but she wasn't very sociable. She seemed lost, she barked all the time. With summer and the number of dogs in the kennel, it wasn't possible to keep her anymore."

"Could you tell me, please, where Daisy is now?"

"José said he sent her to the neighborhood veterinarian, Dr. Durand. I have his number, if you want."

Ferdinand plunges his arm into the yellow bin to retrieve the notebook. For once he's in luck—he finds a pencil inside. He jots down the number, trembling, and hangs up, forgetting to thank the woman. He presses the buttons. Nothing happens. He turns to Mr. Suarez, who shouts, "The green button!" Three rings later, a deep voice on the prerecorded message announces that Ferdinand has indeed reached the veterinarian, but the office is closed during lunch hours. Ferdinand looks at his watch. It's already 12:10.

He'll never be able to wait for two o'clock. And then Marion and Alexandre will be here, and he can't let them down by running to the vet if . . . Ferdinand stops himself from finishing his thought. He returns to the middle of the little garden and sits down next to Mr. Suarez. A glass of port is waiting for him. He looks at it for a moment then asks, "Do you know a veterinarian? A certain Dr. Durand?"

"Yes, quite well. He's Rocco's vet. He works miracles. Our poor baby had a problem with his throat. When he barked he sounded like Rocky. He was ordered not to leave the house to avoid pollution, basically a dog's life. And, well, the doctor's operation changed his life. He barks normally, can walk around town and not even scare the canaries. The poor things, they were hearing a monstrous groan, but didn't see anything coming. They had the jitters! Dr. Durand has even become a friend, at least to my wife. Why do you ask?"

Ferdinand hesitates to share his theory. One, because he doesn't know the end of the story yet. And two, the poor man has just lost his wife—he doesn't need to know how diabolical she was.

"The people at the kennel didn't know much, but they directed me to Dr. Durand. I just tried to call him, but I got his answering machine. Lunch break, apparently. I'm going to have to grin and bear it," says Ferdinand, picking up the glass in front of him.

"I can call him if you like. I have his cell phone number. He'll surely pick up." Mr. Suarez searches through his contact list and nods. "I'm calling him. It's ringing! Yes, Dr. Durand, it's Mr. Suarez. I'm sorry to bother you at lunch but I have a friend who'd like to ask you an important question. Here he is."

Ferdinand seizes the phone, moves some distance away, and explains as calmly as possible how the clues led him there.

***

From afar, Mr. Suarez follows the conversation: a shrug of the shoulder there, a surprised hand gesture there. All of a sudden, the old man seems ill and collapses onto the wall surrounding the courtyard's roses. Ferdinand spasms. He's shaking all over. Mr. Suarez rushes over and asks him what's going on. The old man answers in such a weak voice that the concierge can't understand at first. Then, he manages to read the few words on Ferdinand's lips: "Daisy is alive."

Epilogue

Happy-Go-Lucky

The scene is surreal. Ferdinand's house is crowded, overflowing. Suitcases, bags, noises, words shouted from one room to another, yapping, closet doors banging. From the kitchen where he's cutting a zucchini into slices, which he'll season with a mustard and balsamic vinaigrette (a new recipe from Beatrice), he's trying to get a handle on his emotions. His heart is always pounding. It would really be his luck to pop off now . . . It's decided, he'll buy cod liver oil. He read it's excellent for the heart. Or the memory. He doesn't remember anymore. And then he'll take advantage of his morning at the hospital with Alexandre to visit Dr. Labrousse. A little checkup, just to make sure everything's OK.

While he's dumping the slices into the salad bowl, two pieces escape and fall on the kitchen floor. It doesn't take more than a second for Sherlock, crouching underneath the Formica table, to dart out and gulp it all down. Tail wagging gaily with the regularity of a metronome, he goes back as if nothing had happened, thereby avoiding any scolding. In the living room, he licks his chops in front of a reclining Daisy—queenly, unmoved. Ferdinand can't stop rubbing his eyes. He still doesn't believe it. Daisy is there. So beautiful! So beautiful that some scoundrel got her pregnant. So beautiful that Dr. Durand had wanted to keep her, after she finished nursing her litter of puppies.

That Mrs. Suarez drove him up the wall right until the end. Lying to him to make him fly off the handle. Lying to the kennel by telling them an older gentleman in her complex had suddenly gone for a long stay in the hospital. Lying to her husband. All that just to die without achieving what she really wanted: Ferdinand's departure. As Mr. Suarez concedes, "She wasn't fundamentally evil, just a little pigheaded, sometimes."

Ferdinand decides to visit her grave. It'll be a walk for the dogs. And then it'll be the perfect place to dump the contents of the urn filled with the ashes of a poor Great Dane that Dr. Durand had given to Mrs. Suarez in order to stage her horrible ruse. Why had the veterinarian agreed to such a thing? Ferdinand will never know. He didn't think to ask for explanations when he went to the vet's with Mr. Suarez to implore him to give back his dog. He didn't have to make too many arguments. Daisy's joyous barks and frantic jumping as soon as she heard her old master's voice were sufficient.

Ferdinand takes new plates out from under their protective cloths. He doesn't even have three matching plates. This will do for today, but he'll have to invest in new dishes. He'll ask Madeleine to help him, it being a given that Juliette eats over at his house as often as his daughter and grandson. Oh, Madeleine . . . Ferdinand can't wait to see her again. Even if their relationship is platonic, just being with her, laughing with her, holding her hand, sitting side by side on a bench, does him a world of good.

The caramelized aroma emanating from the oven brings Ferdinand back to reality. He checks on his gratin dauphinois and finds it's crusty on top and well browned, ready for the table. In the kitchen, they're a little cramped. The three occupants are more tired than hungry, and the conversation barely follows any kind of logic. Each is lost in his or her own thoughts: you could hear a fly buzz if Sherlock weren't teasing Daisy.

Alexandre, staring off into space, sees the little beagle nibbling at the big dog's dangling ear. His eyelids are drooping; it's time for him to go to bed. Marion is looking over every nook and cranny in the room. This kitchen, now dated, was her favorite room, always perfumed with the fragrance of flan, warm French toast, or rice pudding. She even surprises herself by noticing the place's undeniable cleanliness.

As for Ferdinand, he's thinking about the long day waiting for him tomorrow. The compatibility test. Even though for him there's nothing worse than medical tests, he's not afraid. He's even serene. He'd really like to do this for his grandson, not out of competition or jealousy. Just because his family needs him, and because, for the first time in his life, he can be useful—he, Ferdinand Brun. He can do something good. For someone else.

Acknowledgments

Although *Out of Sorts* ends here on these pages, the adventure began a little over a year ago, in a café in Milan.

The journey was unusual for a first novel, since it followed the path of self-publication. On a whim, I placed the fate of my manuscript in the hands of unknown readers, to get an honest opinion, but also out of fear—fear of a negative response from established publishers. And that was the book's first step out into the world. All of a sudden, Ferdinand met his audience. Some, touched by the story, wrote to me; they'd laughed, been moved, or had changed their lives somehow after reading, by reaching out to a grumpy loved one, for example. These messages turned my life upside-down more than I'd ever imagined.

Therefore, I'd like to start by addressing my sincerest thanks to the first, anonymous readers of *Out of Sorts*. Without you, these pages could have remained nothing but forgotten sheets covered with inconsequential black lines. I can't mention each person by name, because Ferdinand charmed thousands of readers, but each message I received brought me immense joy and drove me to finish my second novel.

This incredible buzz surrounding a self-published novel attracted the attention of major publishing houses, the same ones I hadn't dared send my manuscript to. With the unwavering support of Anne-Laure Vial and Eric Bergaglia from Amazon KDP France, whose coaching for young self-published authors is invaluable, *Out of Sorts* encountered a fantastic editor, Gabriella Page-Fort, from Amazon Publishing. My thanks to her for her enthusiasm from the very first read-through, for her confidence, and for giving me this magnificent opportunity to achieve a childhood dream. Thanks to Wendeline Hardenberg for her faithful translation—not easy to do with all those "Frenchy" idioms—which will allow the novel to be read in all four corners of the globe, far beyond what I could have imagined. And an enormous thank-you to the whole Amazon Publishing team for their expertise and immeasurable support. You've given another life to our crotchety old Ferdinand.

Finally, the following people have accompanied me throughout this incredible adventure, reading the first drafts full of typos, searching for resemblance to their loved ones, fretting with me over the first few weeks of self-publication as well as at every launch in a new country. Their support means everything to me, and I would be nothing without them: my incredible husband, Olivier; my adorable son, Jules; my best friend and first reader,

Chinda; my parents, Corinne and Michel; my family and friends! From the bottom of my heart, *merci*.

About the Author

Aurélie Valognes was born and raised close to Paris, France. After business school studies, she began working for American companies and spent the early part of her career as a brand manager, working and traveling across Europe. Only when she and her husband had the opportunity to move from their home country for an international assignment in Italy did Aurélie rekindle her love for writing. *Out of Sorts* (originally published as *Mémé dans les orties*) became a bestseller in France. It has been translated into many languages. She lives in Milan with her husband and three-year-old son and is working on her second novel.

For more information, visit:

Website: www.aurelie-valognes.com

Facebook: www.facebook.com/aurelievalognesauteur

Twitter: @ValognesAurelie

About the Translator

Wendeline A. Hardenberg first became curious about translation as an undergrad at Smith College, where she ultimately translated part of a novel from French as a portion of her honors thesis in comparative literature. After receiving a dual master's degree in comparative literature (with a focus on translation) and library science at Indiana University Bloomington, she has gone on to a dual career as a translator and a librarian. Her first translation for AmazonCrossing, Jacques Vandroux's *Heart Collector*, was published in February 2015. Learning new languages and trying to translate from them is one of her favorite hobbies. She lives in New Haven, Connecticut.